THE DEFENDER

#6

ESCAPE

Books by Jerry Ahern

The Survivalist Series
#1: Total War
#2: The Nightmare Begins
#3: The Quest
#4: The Doomsayer
#5: The Web
#6: The Savage Horde
#7: The Prophet
#8: The End is Coming
#9: Earth Fire
#10: The Awakening

The Defender Series
#1: The Battle Begins
#2: The Killing Wedge
#3: Out of Control
#4: Decision Time
#5: Entrapment

They Call Me the Mercenary Series
#1: The Killer Genesis
#2: The Slaughter Run
#3: Fourth Reich Death Squad
#4: The Opium Hunter
#5: Canadian Killing Ground

THE DEFENDER

#6

ESCAPE

JERRY AHERN

SPEAKING VOLUMES, LLC

NAPLES, FLORIDA

2012

THE DEFENDER

#6 ESCAPE

ISBN 978-1-61232-307-7

For Walt Smisson,
electrician, builder, landscaper, and adventurer—
and a heck of a good friend—
all the best to you and yours . . .

CHAPTER ONE

The river had been harder to get to from their doomed twin-engine Beechcraft than David Holden had thought. The undergrowth was denser and the climb downward was steeper than it had seemed to him in the last seconds before he had been forced to set down. With one engine dead, the second one dying, the gunfire of Innocentio Hernandez's drug smugglers and killers had sealed their fate. And Maria, who had helped Holden escape the fortified villa of Hernandez's employer, the Communist Emiliano Ortega de Vasquez, had struck her head during the crash. As the day wore on, her symptoms of concussion—or something worse—became impossible to ignore. She was feeling dizziness, nausea, disorientation, and her vision was blurred.

The growing severity of Maria's condition forced

them to stop and rest when there was no time for either. Hernandez's men had to be close.

Holden sat beside her, shirtless and shivering; his shirt was draped over Maria's shoulders and chest. There could be no fire and the night was cold. "I'll be back, Maria," he whispered, forcing himself to stand as tremors of pain radiated from his abdomen to every part of his body.

Maria whispered halfheartedly, unintelligibly, as Holden touched her shoulder then grabbed up one of the M-16s. He started back over the same rock-strewn jungle path along which they had come an hour before. His abdomen still tormented him as viciously as it had when he first stood. The origin of his agony was the tortures he had suffered at the hands of Dimitri Borsoi before he'd been brought south, here to Peru, by Hernandez and delivered into the hands of Ortega de Vasquez. Ortega de Vasquez's ultimatum had been: Cooperate with the Front for the Liberation of North America, betray the Patriots—or die. Despite the odds against success, there had been no choice for Holden but to try to escape.

And Maria, the prostitute who crossed herself in fear at the very mention of Innocentio Hernandez's name, had become Holden's unexpected ally so she could escape the same fate as the women of Ortega de Vasquez who had gone before—forced into drug addiction, then killed or thrown into the streets of the nearby town he controlled to starve or worse.

Ortega de Vasquez, Holden realized, was the

FLNA's financial jugular. He was at once a leader in the international Communist-controlled terror network that filled the ranks of the FLNA and, at the same time, an integral part of the all-pervasive drug-smuggling operation that funded it.

Holden reached the spot where the trail split upward and steeply downward. He took neither path, but instead slung the M-16 behind him—its metal and plastic parts were cold against the bare skin of his back and shoulders—and started climbing into the rocks that jutted upward here at the crossroads. He was torn with ambivalence—if he saw Hernandez's men, he would know their position; but if they were too close, he would be trapped.

The cabin depressurization alarm sounded and his breath caught in his throat for an instant, despite the bottled air he'd been breathing for the last two minutes.

Geoffrey Kearney gave a last glance under his coverall front, the Smith & Wesson 5904 (chamber empty, as always on a drop, a condition to be rectified the moment he touched down) secure in its borrowed tanker-style chest holster. Kearney stood up, zipped the coverall closed, and closed the harness buckle over his chest. He looked at his chest pack with the dual altimeters and direction-finding instrumentation, then stepped to the open fuselage doorway.

"On green, sir," the voice said in his earpiece.

"On green, Corporal." Kearney nodded perfunctorily, speaking loudly so his transmission could be heard over the rumbling of the black unmarked Canadian Air Force C-141 B Starlifter's four Pratt & Whitney turbojets and the roar of the slipstream. The light was still red. The ruddy-complexioned, carrot-haired corporal—there was more than a trace of the Scot in him—had been quite discreet. No questions about "Why are we flying so close to the United States border, sir? Is this one of those hush-hush operations a fellow always reads about? Why that nonstandard pistol, sir?" None of that, although Kearney almost felt cheated since he'd worked up a neat package of lies. But there was enough lying in his profession, and the opportunity to be spared telling a few more lies was welcome.

Geoffrey Kearney tugged his chute harness with his black-gloved left hand. If the direction finder didn't work and if the winds were strong, he supposed, there was always the possibility of running into D. B. Cooper sitting under some pine tree and counting ill-gotten gains, a big grin on his face. The infamous air pirate had gone down years before in the Pacific Northwest, which was quite a substantial distance from Kearney's own intended drop zone, south-southeast of the junction of the borders of Minnesota, Wisconsin, and the southern shoreline of Lake Superior.

"Green!" A Klaxon sounded, the light over the jump door changed from red to green, and Kearney took a last look behind him. He shrugged his shoulders and shot the young Canadian Air Force corporal a half salute, then jumped into the night, tumbling, spread-eagling arms and legs to stabilize his fall, looking through his wind goggles to the illuminated faces of the altimeters on his chest pack. The needles spun in perfect synchronization. He judged another ten seconds and it would be time to pull the rip cord.

Nine seconds.

He had learned the high-altitude, high-opening technique when it was first developed a few years before, although the acronym for it, "Haho!" sounded like some idiotic greeting.

Three seconds.

The diode telling him his radio navigation finder was working glowed reassuringly. All around him, above and below, was black. The steadily declining altimeter readings and his sense of reason were the only indications that he was falling down, not up or sideways.

One second. Kearney breathed his oxygen and pulled the rip cord.

There was a sudden but not unanticipated violent jerking of his body, the altimeter readings went to hell, his shoulders and chest feeling pressure. He reached up to the guidelines, his eyes glancing at the chest pack. The constellation of eighteen semisynchronous orbiting Navstar satellites some 12,500 miles above him was apparently on the job. His directional finders were giving him readings and he worked the shrouds to bring himself more westerly when a sudden vicelike cold gripped his stomach. He was over open water, had to be.

The coordinates were preset for his drop. All that he had to do was to keep himself going in the right direction for the right amount of time and come down. Too much westerly correction? He didn't think so. The silence except for the billowing of his chutes was maddening. In a high-altitude, low-opening drop, there was always the slipstream around you, and the sense that you controlled everything that happened. Until you opened the chute. If the main chute didn't open and you didn't panic, there would probably be time to deploy the reserve. If that didn't open, it was always possible to attempt manual deployment. It wasn't likely that there would be time to manually open the chute rapidly enough that you didn't go splat, but it was something to do rather than helplessly awaiting the inevitable.

Doing something rather than helplessly awaiting the inevitable was a good way of describing the Patriots, Kearney supposed. The group was an aggregation of military veterans, ex-cops, and private citizens, men and women, who had taken their own laws into their own hands and tried to save the United States from terrorists. Kearney had monitored the events as they occurred, both personally and professionally. The Service, of course, monitored everything. That was one of its jobs. But the newspapers and television had been full of it, news from the United States becoming more a regular feature on the BBC than news concerning home. The terrorists began with power transformer topplings, then more obvious acts of organized sabotage. And for every item the news carried, there were a dozen more his Service knew of from private sources. Kearney had wondered then, as he wondered now, how many more incidents there had really been against U.S. citizens and the Patriots.

Then acts of human-targeted terror began. The attacks at college and university commencement exercises all across the United States, the bombings of bars and restaurants frequented by military service personnel and police, the random acts of violence in shopping centers and banks and hospitals. The body count kept rising.

All in the name of the Front for the Liberation of North America.

The violence spilled out of the United States, across its borders into Mexico and Canada. As if they all studied imbecility at the same school, leaders of all three governments cracked down on the individual rights of their citizens. That this merely played into the hands of the self-styled FLNA revolutionaries made no difference.

The Patriot organization—a chap at the embassy in Washington was the first to hear of it—became a highly mobile, highly effective force against the violence of the FLNA, more effective than organized police or military operations ever seemed to be. In large part, intelligence data indicated, this peculiarity was due to two factors: first, the upper echelons of the police and military were obviously infiltrated, hence able to alert the FLNA concerning any operations being mounted against them; second, the Patriots were the beneficiaries of military and police intelligence data, even some personnel and equipment. That recently there had been some sort of alliance between the Patriots and the White House seemed obvious, with the FBI and its director, Rudolph Cerillia, as liaison.

All of that was now changed.

Kearney began tacking toward the south, reassured by the altimeter readings from his chest pack. He mentally balanced time against distance and checked his coordinates. So far, so good.

The FLNA had achieved an enormous coup. Using stolen antitank missiles, the FLNA launched an attack against an international security conference whose sole purpose was to determine how to combat the FLNA threat. As a result of the attack, the Vice President of the United States, by all accounts a good man, was dead. The President of the United States was in a coma from which informed sources seemed confident he would never awaken. The Speaker of the House, Roman Makowski, his record as a sycophantic and power-hungry politician unblemished by any trace of higher purpose other than his own reelection, had assumed the presidency. And now, according to the most recent data transmitted to Kearney from London and what cooperating Canadian officials were able to confirm, Makowski was systematically and quickly dismantling the administration of the comatose, near-dead President. His first step had been placing FBI director Cerillia on suspension and under very thinly disguised house arrest. The clandestine FBI task force that intelligence data strongly suggested had been formed to effect cooperation between the Patriots and the White House was dismantled.

When he'd learned that he was actually in the British Secret Intelligence Service (he'd been working in SIS without knowing it, believing he was involved merely in some nonstandard duties in military intelligence), Kearney had hoped there really was some Ian Flemingesque head of the Secret Service—gray eyes, admiral's demeanor, and all. But there was not. So he contented himself with the thought that perhaps at one time there had been. There were, in fact, several men who were empowered to dispatch him to various and sundry ends of the earth when needed, most of the time bikini-clad femmes fatale were in short supply, violent megalomaniacs never surfaced, and, generally, things were rather boring. Yet there were always those rare moments.

Although field assignments most often translated to supervising indigenous intelligence gatherers, compiling reports, checking on supervisory personnel, or some other standard things, there were those moments.

And this was one of them.

One of the usual men who assigned him his duties had called him at home, a rarity. "Could you come round to my club this afternoon, Kearney? I know it's Saturday and all, but something rather interesting has surfaced and you might want to be in on it." It was the sort of invitation he couldn't have resisted if he'd tried.

A late lunch at the fellow's club was followed by a long drive and a walk in the countryside. "We want you to get on top of this Front for the Liberation of North America thing, Kearney. Get the feel of the whole show. Take as long as you need. Then find some way of getting yourself next to the chap who's at the top. However you think best, perhaps insinuating yourself into their very organization. Any resources you might require will be at your complete disposal, of course. Once you're certain of your target, then take the appropriate steps to, ahh—"

The phrase that floated on the air between them, a phrase Kearney detested because of its staginess, was "terminate with extreme prejudice." No one actually told anyone to go out and murder someone else these days, it just floated between them.

The Navstar net's navigational beacons, broadcasting at 26,750 megahertz, were telling his instruments he was less than a mile from his target. Mechanically, his eyes had been scanning the terrain as soon as it became visible. Woodlands, small lakes, highways, farmhouses. There was one particular farmhouse he was looking for. He switched on the auxiliary direction finder. It channeled a signal in the 750-MHz range into his radio, a steady beeping in his ear, the beeping getting increasingly louder and more defined. He worked his lines to bring himself slightly southward. He knew touchdown was imminent. But each second he was able to stay aloft meant less distance to travel on foot. Trees, unexpectedly high. Kearney tugged at his lines, swinging his feet away toward a clearing or maybe just a cow pasture.

He aimed his body toward it, skimming over the lower trees at the boundary of the stand, running as his feet touched, falling to his knees, rolling as the chute started to drag. He hit the emergency release, shrugged out of the harness, and rolled up onto his knees, his right hand moving toward his coverall front as his left hand tore the zipper downward.

The pistol. He left hand racked the S&W's blue-black slide, chambering a round. Then his left hand swept upward, pulling the mask from his face. He inhaled a little too deeply, a light-headed sensation washing over him. But then he was to his feet, albeit a bit unsteadily. His right thumb worked the hammer-drop safety down then up, the hammer at rest but the safety off for a first-round double-action pull, safer than a cocked pistol in darkness over unfamiliar terrain.

He shook his head, the nausea passing. He ran after his chute, caught it, dropped to his knees, tugged it back into the treeline after him, then sat back on his haunches against a tree trunk.

He looked at his chest pack. He was roughly a quarter mile from the farmhouse.

Kearney balled the parachute array and stuffed it in the notch between two trees growing out of the same common trunk, then reached to his thigh and zipped open a leg pouch. There was a locator button there. He affixed it to the packing for his chutes and activated it. The man in the farmhouse could retrieve the chute array and dispose of it at his leisure. The power source had a seventy-two-hour life expectancy in temperatures above freezing. He glanced at his watch. Almost exactly midnight and the temperature readout on his chest pack registered in the lower fifties Fahrenheit. So much for freezing temperatures.

He shrugged out of the chest pack, all systems off. Then he hand-wired the destruct mechanism together, tested it, satisfied. Looking from side to side, Kearney moved deeper into the woods, finding a small clearing about ten feet in diameter a hundred yards or so in.

He put the chest pack at the clearing's center, then activated the destruct mechanism. There was a thirty-second delay, long enough for him to get well back. There would be a flash and the possibility of a small fire from the instrumentation in the package frying. The flash came, with it the smell of burning insulation, a flare of flame for the briefest instant, and then a small cloud of acrid-smelling smoke enveloped the pack. No matter who found it now, it would look like nothing more than a mass of burned electronic parts.

As he walked back toward the cow pasture,

threading his way through the trees, he mentally patted himself down. The Smith & Wesson 9mm, two spare twenty-round magazines, and one standard fourteen-round magazine, two Case-Guard fifty-round ammunition boxes, like the magazines loaded with Federal 115-grain Jacketed Hollow-Point 9mm BPs, the two knives, one a little ballpoint pen-size B&D Grande in natural stainless finish, the other a subdued black B&D Fazendeiro, as versatile and reliable a lockblade folding knife as he'd ever owned, were all in their proper places. Identification, credit cards, money. Everything else he'd need would be at the farmhouse.

Kearney hoped.

From the breast pocket of his coveralls he took the solitary 9mm Parabellum round he'd removed from the 5904's chamber before takeoff just north of Thunder Bay, Ontario. He removed the magazine up the autoloader's butt, inserted that single round beneath the feed lips, and pushed it to the rear, then whacked the spine of the magazine against the gloved palm of his hand. He replaced the magazine. The 5904 was a standard pistol, fixed sights and all, nothing to distinguish it from any other of its type except that one of the SIS gunsmiths had taken out the rear sight at Kearney's request and neutralized the magazine safety below it, then replaced the rear sight. Now the pistol would fire a single shot if need be even if no magazine was available and, more to the point, it could still fire while a tactical magazine change was being made.

Back at the V-notch between the double trunks,
Kearney set the pistol down on his parachute array
and quickly doffed his coveralls, chilled in the first
few seconds despite the heavy black cotton fatigue
sweater he wore. He transferred his few personal
items—Zippo lighter, cigarettes, and so on—from
the coverall pockets to the pockets of his black
jeans. From the haversack where his spare ammunition and extra cigarettes were, he extracted the goat-
skin A-2 bomber jacket and, after shaking it out,
slipped it on. Also from the haversack, Kearney
took his holster for the 5904, then inserted the pistol
and clipped the holster inside his waistband.

The farmhouse.

He caught up the haversack and started for it
across the pasture.

There were torches burning about a half-mile dis-
tant, the night incredibly clear, perhaps because it
was so cold. He spotted torches and the smaller,
straighter beams of flashlights. Headlights were visible as well, jostling above the rough track that paralleled the river for about a mile, looping down from
the mountains and then back across the valley.
Comparing the apparent height of the torches to the
headlights, it seemed likely some of the torchbearers
were mounted on horses.

Holden had no doubts that, by morning, there
would be searchplanes looking for them. By then
they had to have reached the river and gotten past
the roadway where the searchers now traveled. It

would be risking Maria's life under the circumstances, but to remain would be assuring her death.

Holden, despite his exhaustion, despite the continuous dull throb in his stomach, realized he was smiling.

Maria, "the prostitute with the heart of gold" indeed.

David Holden started down out of the rocks.

The farmhouse showed only one light in an upstairs window, casting a dull yellow glow. Geoffrey Kearney walked slowly, staying toward the barn side of the yard, giving himself time to react and cover to reach if necessary. But there was no mistaking the origin of the little homing beacon he'd picked up. The house even matched the photograph he'd been shown. The people who lived there were Patriots with strong ties to Canada. In the early days of the Patriot movement—weeks were like months, months like years in this struggle, Kearney knew—Patriots sought by United States authorities had taken refuge across the border, living under assumed names until it was safe to return. Some still lived like this. The man who owned this farmhouse —Hiram Wallenstein—was the conductor for this underground railroad.

Kearney stopped before the porch steps, prepared to ascend them. The door opened and Kearney dodged left over the railing as he drew his pistol. He hit the hedgerow, rolled out of it, and came up on his knees as a shotgun muzzle swung toward him. A woman's voice. "Are you a stranger?"

Kearney's finger eased its pressure on the Smith & Wesson's trigger. "That's a situation easily remedied."

"It's dangerous for strangers alone around here."

"It's dangerous everywhere in times like these." Although the code phrase exchange was complete, Kearney still didn't holster his pistol. He was supposed to be met by a man. "Who are you?"

"I'm Hiram Wallenstein's daughter. He won't be making it."

Kearney approached the porch rail, his haversack in his left hand, the gun in his right, its muzzle angled downward. She had soft-looking hair, long and dark, flowing past her slight shoulders, the shoulders hunched under a blanket shawl, the shawl incongruous-looking considering the rest of her ensemble—T-shirt, blue jeans, and house slippers made to look like the feet of some hairy monster, claws and all.

"I'm Peter Lynch," he lied, giving her the name she expected. "Why won't your father be making it?"

"There was never much law up here, but nobody ever needed much. When the FLNA came, they tried making themselves the law. Every policeman that came up here died or wished he had. That's why so many of us became Patriots. Self-defense. The FLNA almost controls this whole part of the state, and parts of your country too. They hit a Patriot meeting. Poppa and three other men and a woman and her baby were killed last night. There wasn't any time to change plans, everything happened so fast."

He still didn't holster his gun. "What's your name?"

"Harriet."

"Harriet," Kearney repeated.

"Don't make any jokes about Ozzie."

"Ozzie?"

"You know—Ozzie and Harriet and David and Ricky?"

"Ohh—the thing on the television, yes. I always liked *Garden Party* best myself."

"Me too. I got your stuff, Mr. Lynch."

"Peter, please."

"Come in out of the cold. There's my poppa's scotch if you got a mind to, or coffee or hot chocolate."

"Hot chocolate would be wonderful, then perhaps a glass of your father's whiskey. I'm sorry for you, terribly."

"When Poppa heard the Canadians were sending somebody in, he said, 'Lay you even money, he's one of those British agents and they want to kill the guy who runs the FLNA.' "

Kearney prided himself on handling matters calmly, but he was taken aback. After all, her father was dead. So, as enigmatically as he could, he told her, "Your father seems to have been marvelously astute," then started up the steps.

"Is Peter your real name, Mr. Lynch?" She lowered her shotgun, Kearney noticing without trying to that it was a Remington 870 and a 12 gauge.

"No. But Peter will do. I had a very good friend named Peter once. So I wouldn't mind you calling me by that name, not at all."

"Peter."

"Harriet."

"Come inside."

Kearney kept his gun in his hand as he followed her inside. She was lovely—he had ample proof of that as he caught a glimpse of her face in the light of a lamp, an almost fragile quality in her features— and he was sorry for the death of her father. But he wasn't twelve years old anymore either.

David half carried Maria, concentrating on the cold that assailed their bodies so he could keep himself from thinking about the cramps in his stomach. Oddly, the exercise seemed to be helping him. They had tortured him with a method perfected years before, using automobile batteries to inflict electric shocks to his body, then all but drowning him in ice-cold water, then beating the water from his body with boards struck across his abdomen; then electrocution again. And the purpose to all of it had simply been to cause him pain.

Borsoi.

If—when—when he got back, he would find Borsoi and pay him back. No torture. Just a bullet or a knife.

As he felt Maria's body against him, Holden's mind suddenly filled with images of Rosie Shepherd. After his wife, Elizabeth, had been murdered in the FLNA attack on Thomas Jefferson University, their children murdered as well, Holden had told himself he would never love anyone again. Then, without wanting to, he'd fallen in love again. Rosie Shepherd.

If somehow she hadn't escaped the trap Borsoi had set for him, killing Borsoi wouldn't be enough.

Was the President still clinging to life? What about Luther Steel and the men of his Metro Task Force, Clark Pietrowski, Bill Runningdeer, Tom LeFleur, and Randy Blumenthal?

Holden and Maria moved down along a rocky defile, the loose shale underfoot making movement torturously slow and, with the slightest misstep, betrayingly noisy. The road was off to their left and well below them still, but he heard voices and stopped, hugging Maria close to him as she slumped in his arms.

The hot chocolate was the good kind, not made from a prepared packet but with milk heated in a saucepan on the four-burner electric stove in the modern but modest kitchen at the rear of the farmhouse. The kitchen had gleaming tile and counters and neatly arranged pots and pans and a drainboard half filled with spotless dishes, despite the dishwasher evident to the side of the sink. Walking through the living room into the kitchen was like walking from one era into another. The living room —or perhaps it was more appropriately called a great room—was dominated by an enormous hearth, the size of some he'd seen in old English country houses. Above the hearth was a percussion rifle, a Hawken, a powder horn and a ditty bag slung near it. Alongside were three deer heads, meticulously mounted. At first, Kearney had thought the walls were paneled, then he realized as he drew nearer to the hearth that the walls were made of logs, the hearth made of real flagstones.

It was a fine house, albeit emptier tonight.

"The hot chocolate is very good, Harriet."

"I'll get you that glass of scotch," she offered, just finishing washing out the saucepan and setting it in the drainboard with the rest of the dishes. "Could I make you a sandwich or heat up something?"

"No, really—I ate not terribly long ago."

She nodded, wiped her hands on the print apron she wore, then untied it, setting it on the counter. She left the kitchen, returning after a moment with the bottle of the whiskey she, like all Americans it seemed, called scotch. It was a brand he didn't recognize, and although he was always wary of that sort of thing he was committed to trying it.

Without saying a word, she walked to one of the overhead cabinets and took down a whiskey tumbler. "Ice?"

"No—neat is fine."

She set the tumbler on the table, then left the kitchen again. Kearney finished his hot chocolate while he examined the bottle. Its origins dubious, he sniffed at the open mouth as he set the cap on the table. Shrugging, he poured a half-inch of the liquid into the tumbler, then set down the bottle and capped it. He swirled the liquid in the bottom of the glass, still doing so when Harriet Wallenstein returned. She was carrying what looked like a large sewing basket. She set it on the table, whatever was inside it apparently heavy. She furled back a half-finished piece of embroidery work and one by one emptied the basket of its contents. Two green plastic MTM Case-Guard boxes, but these the larger, hundred-round variety. One standard-length magazine for his pistol. A cleaning kit, one of the universal-size ones designed to work with most commonly encountered calibers in long guns or handguns. A small block of cedar that he recognized as housing a set of ceramic sharpening sticks. A black-handled Cold Steel Trailmaster Bowie knife. One of the double-edged Terminator push daggers, also made by Cold Steel. There were assorted other items, and, as she laid them on the table, she told him, "There's an assault rifle and ammunition and spare magazines and everything and some other things, but I had to spread things around a little so I could hide them. And the car is parked in the barn. How are you ever going to get across state lines with this stuff?"

He raised the glass of whiskey near to his lips, saying "Here's to careless state police border inspections!" And he tossed back the whiskey. It was actually quite satisfactory. "The car is specially modified so I can hide these things rather well. Shouldn't be much bother, really."

"You are going to kill somebody?"

Kearney said nothing, not wanting to lie to her, unable to let out more information than he already had. "Will you join me?" He gestured toward the bottle. She picked it up, opened it, and, for a second, Kearney thought she was going to drink straight out of the bottle, but instead she poured another inch of the liquid into his glass. "I hate scotch. But I'll have a beer." She walked to the refrigerator as he closed the bottle. "You smoke?"

"Yes."

"Thought so with the carton of cigarettes they sent along." Kearney was grateful the RCMP chap had remembered. "Light up if you want. I'll get an ashtray. Poppa used snuff."

What a delightful habit. Kearney smiled, saying nothing. "But every once in a while, he'd smoke a cigar. When do you have to leave?"

"I don't think I'm supposed to leave until morning," Kearney answered as noncommittally as he could.

"Good." She set the ashtray down. Kearney lit a Pall Mall with his Zippo, setting cigarettes and lighter on the table amid the contents of the sewing basket. "They certainly gave you some good stuff." She gestured toward the knives and ammunition and accessories with her beer bottle.

"My own things, for the most part. But if everything goes well, I'll probably never need them."

"You're more the subtle type?"

He smiled, hardly ever having thought of himself as subtle. "What do you do? I mean, when you're not making hot chocolate and glasses of whiskey for strangers?"

"I used to teach school, but the little school is closed. The parents were afraid to send their children after the bus was attacked."

"A school bus?"

"Firebombed. FLNA."

Kearney shook his head, staring at the whiskey tumbler. Madness.

"Did you say something?"

"No—but I was thinking that this is madness. I mean, one doesn't expect this sort of thing in the United States. Ulster, the Middle East, some of the African or Asian states, of course, it's an unfortunate fact of life. But not here. So—you can't teach anymore because they closed the school."

"Poppa took me in. He was sore at me when I married Tom."

Kearney had been about to sip at his drink, but he stopped, saying to her "Then you're not alone at least."

"Tom was always kind of radical. Maybe that was what attracted me to him in college. He was always against the government, the police, against gun ownership, against big business, all that stuff. Poppa called him a 'damned commie' and that made me sore. Poppa and I fought. Poppa came to the wedding, said he would never do something like stay away; but he told me I was stupid for marrying Tom. Poppa was right. Tom's gone now."

"I'm—" Kearney started to offer condolences for the double tragedy in her life.

"He's not dead; he's just gone. He's with the FLNA. For all I know, he helped firebomb that schoolbus or even helped kill Poppa. That's why I moved back in with Poppa. When they killed those children, I, ahh—" She took a hard pull on the bottle of beer and it was empty. She seemed to be looking around for a place to put the bottle. Kearney reached out and took it from her hand.

Innocentio Hernandez was not among them. Six men, two of them on horseback, the other four carrying torches or flashlights, were moving along a wider track, perhaps a long-used animal trail that ran parallel to the shale-strewn defile David Holden and Maria had walked along and beside which they now hid. The animal trail and the six men who moved along it were a hundred yards below. Maria moaned in pain beside him, dry heaves having plagued her since they'd moved on again. Her brow was feverish and her eyes slightly glassy-looking when last he'd dared use a light to look.

The horses could mean the difference between life and death for her, between reaching the river and somehow getting below the trail or never reaching it at all. There were blankets behind the cantles of the two saddles and all six men wore heavy coats.

Holden shifted aside two of the M-16s, slinging the third muzzle down and crossbody from left shoulder to right side, chamber loaded. His right thumb found the safety tumbler and he moved it to auto. Holden whispered to Maria, not knowing if she understood him anymore, "I'll be back. Be very quiet. Don't be frightened when you hear gunfire." Had this been some slick adventure film instead of reality, there would have been some unique and ultimately effective way of taking out the six men one at a time and silently. Instead, he would have to rely on gunning them down, corraling their horses, and getting Maria and himself as far away as possible before any other of Innocentio Hernandez's men came to investigate the shooting.

And there was at least one radio. He could hear the crackle of static; the squelch was not working properly or was improperly adjusted.

Holden took the Remington 870 into his fists. His training as a police officer while he'd finished graduate school had inculcated him into the habit of never making a shotgun hot before absolutely necessary. And so the pump was chamber empty, six rounds still in the tubular magazine.

He was up, moving back along the shale-strewn defile as silently as he could. The direction of movement of the six men was up the mountain, not down. If he hurried and was lucky, he could cut them off—the lucky part was really important.

* * *

Suddenly it had just happened. Their hands touched. The tears that she must have held back at the death of her father—Poppa—came. She came into his arms and Geoffrey Kearney held her tightly.

After a long time of standing there, she kissed him, at first softly, hesitantly. And when he kissed her, she clung to him and her mouth searched his and she whispered, "Make love to me, please—"

Kearney slipped between her legs, his hands touching at her gently. Rolling into bed with a girl he'd just met was not his habit, but there was an urgency in her and somehow he felt it too. She was so touched by death, they both needed the reassurance of life. She was awkward as she touched him, brought him inside her. And she held him so tightly that the muscles in his neck began to cramp.

He rolled over, bringing her on top of him, his fingers touching gently at her breasts. She started to move, her body rhythm something that was at once independent of them both and part of them.

Kearney rolled over on top of her, without separating from her. She arched her back upward, her abdomen pressing tight against his. He forced her voice from his mind as he came inside her, her body trembling, her lips murmuring the name he'd given her as his, "Peter." Peter was the name of the first man he had ever killed, and some fool in documents or some fool above the documents section—or maybe it was only coincidence without malevolent intent—had given him that name for the mission. But hearing it reminded him of death and Kearney didn't want to be reminded of death now—not at all.

The abdominal pains were such a part of his existence now that he hardly noticed them unless he thought about them. David Holden reached the high point of rocks where he had originally gone to look out on the terrain below them. The six men, two on horseback, were still coming up the parallel trail. The rocks rose over the trail some twenty feet, a spit of rock extending outward so far that it nearly formed a natural portico over the trail. Doubtless, in times of heavy rains, travelers along the trail would have used the rock overhang as protection.

Holden's plan was simple. Cut the men down with the M-16 as quickly as he could, then jump down, using the shotgun to quickly finish them. There would be no time to check which of them were dead or alive. He merely had the time—if he was lucky—to jump down, rack the pump, and put one load of Double O Buckshot into the head of each man. It provided little comfort that they would have done the same to him.

He could hear the clopping of the horses' hooves on the shale, hear the murmurings of the six men, sounding disgruntled. It was a long and cold night. At last Holden saw the flickering of one of the torches, then the yellow beam of a flashlight.

Holden set the pump shotgun carefully, silently

on the flat rock surface beside him. He drew the Defender knife, shifting the sheathless blade to the small of his back so that, if he fell on it, there would be less possibility of injury to himself. Slowly he shifted the M-16 forward, his palms sweating, the naked flesh of his upper body so cold he trembled. Crouched there at the edge of the rock overhang, David Holden waited. . . .

Kearney heard the sound only once, but once was enough. His right arm was around Harriet Wallenstein. Tom, her husband, had to have been a rotter; she was back to using her maiden name. But, of course, she hadn't said that, actually, merely said her name was Harriet and that she was Wallenstein's daughter. His right arm was tingling a little as he moved it. But his left hand was already closed over the butt of the Smith & Wesson 9mm, his left thumb working the ambidexterous safety up and off. Someone or something was moving in the great room beyond the small hallway off which her bedroom was located.

Kearney closed his right hand over Harriet's mouth and whispered in her ear, her eyes going wide open at the first syllable of his first word. "There's someone in the house. Remain perfectly quiet. Slip off the bed on my side. Wrap the blanket around you or something. Nod if you understand. And remember—" She nodded. "—be perfectly quiet."

Kearney rolled over the side of the bed, suddenly

naked, suddenly cold. Harriet came over after him, pulling the quilt with her, coccooning herself inside it as she knelt beside him. Kearney pushed her forward and down, almost flat on the floor by the head of the bed. He edged toward the foot of the bed, hearing another footfall. Closer this time. He caught up his underpants from the pile on the chair, skinned into them, shifted his pistol to his right hand. There was no time to pull on his jeans.

The door opened. "Harriet?" The man was tall, lean, the face classically handsome except for the eyes. There were more kinds of evil in them than Kearney had thought one man could possess. "We're burning the house as an example to the damn Patriots. Get out while—"

Kearney's eyes flickered from the man in the doorway to Harriet. She was on her knees now, the quilt caught up in a tiny, white-knuckled fist between her breasts. She hissed, "Tom."

Tom's right hand rose, an M-16 coming from beside his right thigh. "Bitch!"

Geoffrey Kearney stabbed the Smith & Wesson toward Tom, Harriet's husband, squinting his eyes against the muzzle flashes to come. Their comparative brilliance to the darkness to which his eyes had become accustomed would be blinding. He double-actioned the 9mm once, then three quick single-action follow-up shots, stitching a line of gradually reddening bullet holes across Tom's chest and neck and left cheek and forehead, the FLNA man—the irate husband—falling back against the partially open door, the door vibrating under his body weight, his body slipping down along its length, his eyes wide open.

Kearney expected a shriek in the next instant. All Harriet said was "He deserved it."

Kearney stepped onto the bed and over it, catching up the M-16. There was no need to check Tom, her husband. If he wasn't dead, he was a fantastic impressionist. "Fetch my pants and my shoes and the rest of my things. Get yourself dressed. Quickly." Kearney peered into the hallway, saw no one, heard no one, and stepped out and across into the partially open bathroom doorway.

He checked the hallway again, shrugged, moved to the toilet and urinated, not flushing. Back to the doorway. He caught up the M-16 he'd leaned there. If no one had come rushing in yet, it meant either good professional caution on the part of the FLNA enemy outside or that Tom had come ahead to get Harriet out before the main body of FLNA personnel arrived. There was a third alternative, of course —that no FLNA housewarming was scheduled at all and Tom had merely used that as a ruse to get next to his estranged wife, for good or for bad.

Harriet, dressed in the same blue jeans and T-shirt but with track shoes on instead of the furry monster slippers, was in the bedroom doorway. There was a revolver stuffed in the front of her jeans, half visible where the T-shirt caught on it. "My pants," Kearney hissed. She tossed the black jeans across to him. Kearney slipped them on, leaving them open. She threw him his gray shirt and he shifted his pistol around as he got into it. The black fatigue sweater. He tied it over his shoulders tennis fashion, zipping his pants, closing the belt, stuffing the autoloader into his waistband.

Kearney caught up the M-16, whispering across the hallway to her, "Stay right behind me but not too close. Leave that revolver where you've got it unless you need it." Kearney stepped into the hallway, checking his pockets for ID, money, his lighter. His cigarettes were on the kitchen table beside the sewing basket, the sewing basket repacked and covered. His leather jacket remained on the chair back.

Kearney stepped into the hallway. Harriet started to cross over to his side but Kearney waved her back. It was a short hallway and only a few steps took them into the entranceway to the great room. No one was in evidence, nothing seemed disturbed. Kearney ran into the room and ducked behind the massive old sofa, from where he was able to look into the kitchen and onto the front porch. His eyes well accustomed to the darkness again after the muzzle flashes from his pistol, he could see reasonably well. But again he saw no one.

He started for the kitchen, Harriet falling in behind him. The basket was where they'd left it, the A-2 jacket as well. With Harriet beside him, Kearney checked the entire house. There was no basement, no second floor. "There's a cellar, but they wouldn't be down there. It doesn't lead into the house," she told him.

No one in the front yard or the backyard.

The M-16 across his lap, his sweater going on the right way as he spoke, Kearney sat her down on the floor behind the couch where he could see both yards and both doors. "I'm sorry I had to kill your husband."

"I'm not. He was a shit. How many innocent people has he killed with the lousy FLNA? Think how many lives you just saved. The world's better off without him. I would have killed him if I could have. Maybe not as efficiently. He was responsible for the schoolbus bombing. I always knew that. He was a child murderer."

Kearney changed the subject. "If he was telling the truth, they're coming here to burn your house. The choice is up to you. Either in the next two minutes gather your belongings and get in that car with me and I'll get you to safety; or wait with me and we'll stop them when they show up. I'm open to either option, Harriet."

"Then we'll wait for them."

Kearney exhaled slowly, softly. "All right," he said.

The six men were almost directly under the natural rock portico. David Holden knew enough to wait and shoot them all in the back. In his youth, reared on a diet of cowboy movies and superheroes, only the evil villain shot people in the back. But he couldn't remember a single one of the stories where a helpless woman would die if the good guy failed, or a story where the bad guys involved had been drug smugglers, murderers, terrorists, and Communists.

As the six men, the two on horseback to the rear, cleared the portico of rock, David Holden came up to his knees, cheeking the M-16 and firing.

A three- or four-round burst into the back of the nearest horseman. Under other circumstances, he would have shot the men farthest away first, but the horsemen had better chances of getting away and the horses—at least one of them—were vital to getting Maria to the river. Holden swung the muzzle on line with the second horseman as the first spilled from the saddle, the animal rearing wildly under him. Holden fired, another short burst into the second horseman's back.

Holden shifted the muzzle left. One of the torchbearers with a submachine gun was swinging the muzzle upward toward Holden's position. His body was half turned toward Holden as Holden fired, the body continuing to turn, the submachine gun discharging into the darkness. Holden shifted the muzzle again. A second torchbearer. Holden triggered a burst that caught the man in the abdomen, jackknifing his body forward as his legs snapped out from under him and he dropped.

Gunfire.

Holden fired toward its source.

More gunfire. The rocks near Holden's right knee

powdered. Holden fired again, a long burst of assault rifle fire shooting skyward, then into the ground. A flashlight rolled across the ground. A horse vaulted between Holden and the sixth man. Assault rifle fire tore into the rocks beside Holden. As the horse cleared his line of sight, Holden fired. He fired a second burst and a third, the M-16 empty.

There was no answering gunfire.

Holden changed magazines, cycled the action, looked over the side of the rock portico as he grabbed up the shotgun. He dropped, coming down in a roll and spilling forward onto the ground, the wind knocked out of him. He lay there for an instant, telling himself all of this was insane. He was killing men he'd never met. He was lost in some godforsaken wilderness in South America. The woman he loved was fighting for her life all alone. A woman who had helped him was dying.

Why did Elizabeth and the children have to die? Life had been so good—why?

He was up to his knees, tromboning the pump shotgun, the head of the first of the six men less than ten yards from him. Holden fired from hip level, closing his eyes as he stood up. The next nearest man. Holden fired again.

Methodically Holden moved about the ground below the rock portico, the horses whinnying maddeningly. He couldn't risk grabbing for the horses as long as one of the six might be alive and armed.

The shotgun was nearly empty.

The sixth man.

"Hey, *amigo—por favor,* huh? Do not—"

"Shut the fuck up," David Holden whispered, suddenly very weary. He pulled the trigger and turned his back. He had to get the horses.

When they entered the barn, he saw the car. But he still saw Harriet's husband, Tom, walking into the bedroom. It was the sort of thing that he wouldn't forget for a long time, if he ever did. No matter that the man was in thick with the Front for the Liberation of North America. No matter that he was probably a mass murderer, a traitor to his country, a saboteur, a cold-blooded terrorist killer. It mattered, but—after all, the man had found him—Kearney—sleeping with his wife.

If the fellow had come with reconciliation in his heart, then why the gun? But why had he come at all? If this Tom was as bad a chap as his wife painted him to be, then why had he come to warn her out of the farmhouse before his FLNA friends burned it to the ground around her ears?

The car was just as anticipated, a current model Ford LTD, but under the hood it carried the full police interceptor package and the suspension, he assumed, was as asked for as well, built for rough driving at high speeds. While Harriet was looking the other way, he made a quick inspection, ascertaining that the special compartments had indeed been worked into the car that would allow him to smuggle weapons across state lines with relative impunity. A smart customs inspector used to wily drug smugglers and the like might find his contraband weapons, but the average policeman wouldn't.

The assault rifle provided for him was a Colt, semiautomatic only (if caught, he'd rather be hanged for a lamb than a sheep any day), the collapsible stock version of the M-16, the CAR-15.

He gave the Ford a test start. If more of the FLNA people than he anticipated should arrive, he might need the car in a hurry. While behind the wheel, he did a one-sided radio check. The citizens band unit worked perfectly well on receive. There was no way to check if he was sending properly because such a transmission might be intercepted by the FLNA.

He went to stand with Harriet beside the barn door. The sky was getting just faintly gray in the east. He wondered, smiling at the thought, if the Front for the Liberation of North America might at all be like American Indians of the movies and attack at dawn. His plan was a simple one, that the enemy would be concentrating on burning the house and ignore the barn for the time being. If the numbers worked out properly, he could take care of the rest.

Harriet spoke. "Are you sorry?"

"I say?"

"Are you sorry?"

"For shooting your husband? I already told you that, and then you told me I shouldn't—"

"No," she said, whispering, her voice sounding odd. "I mean, for us. What we did."

"No—I could never be sorry for that. Are you?"

"No. It's the best thing that happened to me since I fell in with Tom. After we'd make love—and it was just him, really. He never really cared what I wanted. I'd try to tell him what I wanted sometimes, but he never listened. I mean, his eyes never listened, you know? After we'd make love—"

"You don't really have to tell me this," Kearney almost implored.

"After, he'd always talk about his plans, his plans for when the people—he never said who they were —but when the people were in power. The rich had been rich long enough. Those who survived the takeover would be stripped of their wealth. Let them see how it felt to beg. Land, wealth, everything would be redivided, equally."

"Pretty standard Communist line, really. I don't think even the Communists much care for it anymore, certainly not the Chinese, and it looks as though the Russians have been coming around a bit of late as well. The only true Marxists are the revolutionaries. They're the only ones who can afford the luxury of championing a system that history's proven doesn't work."

"What if the FLNA wins?" Harriet asked him.

"Everyone loses; oddly enough, the real hardline thinkers in the FLNA would lose most of all. Nothing more bitter than a disillusioned idealist, Harriet."

He could have used sound and light grenades, a disposable rocket launcher or two. But he'd have to make do, he and Harriet, Harriet with her Winchester lever action .30–30 and her .38 Special revolver, and he with his Colt rifle and Smith & Wesson handgun.

The dead men's clothes were bloodied and ventilated with bullet holes, but David Holden had no open wounds and would risk contact with their blood for the warmth of their coats. He took the best two he could find, wearing one, lashing the other to the second horse as he mounted the first. Catching the animals had consumed the better part of twenty minutes. Along with the clothing, he'd relieved the bodies of any other useful items—ammunition in compatible calibers, flashlights, an unopened Milky Way bar, and, most important, a compass. It was an Asian copy of the standard G.I. Lensatic model, but it would serve under the circumstances.

There had been no sign of any more of Innocentio Hernandez's men coming to the sounds of the gunfire, and the radio traffic from the hand-held transmitter had been pretty standard or, mostly, nonexistent.

Mounted, tugging the second animal after him, David Holden risked the wider and faster animal trail, a flashlight handy but not turned on. Riding horseback was something he hadn't done in years. He hoped it was like riding a bicycle. But he remembered the last time he'd ridden a bicycle. It hadn't been much fun and he hadn't been much good at it. He had not seen the faces of any of the six men he had cut down; that was probably a good thing. He had talked with his son, Dave, one time about what so very much troubled him now. "What did you want to be when you grew up, Dad?"

"What do you mean?"

"I mean, what did you want to be?"

"Well, I guess that depends on what age I was at. When I was really little—your little sister's age—I wanted to be the Lone Ranger or Captain Midnight. My whole life kind of revolved around Cheerios and Ovaltine."

"Cheerios and Ovaltine?"

"Sometimes, some Wheaties. The Reverend Bob Richards was a pole-vaulting champion and I kind of liked his style. He did what people had pretty much said was impossible."

"This guy was on the cereal box?"

"Yeah. So I guess I wanted to be a crime fighter who alternately rode around on a white horse or flew in a jet plane and pole vaulted on the side. That make any sense?"

"Yeah. No—but you wanted to be a good guy. Nobody grows up to be a good guy, like on television or in the movies."

"Maybe, my man, the reason nobody grows up to be a good guy anymore is because everybody says nobody grows up to be a good guy. Know what I mean?"

"Yeah, but—ahh—whatever—"

"Right. You gonna be a good guy?"

"Nobody rides around on a white horse."

"Sure—some people do. Maybe it just looks like a police car or a tank or a fire truck or something, but it's really a white horse, or a jet plane."

David Holden closed his eyes, wondering what Dave would have thought of him now, if the boy could have seen what he had done back at the rock portico. He—David Holden—could have given his son reasons for killing the six men, and very valid ones too. But shooting men down like that wasn't the good-guy thing to do. And David Holden wondered, now, if somewhere along the line since this thing with the FLNA began—he wondered if somewhere along the line, his white horse and his jet plane had gotten lost.

CHAPTER TWO

He hadn't quite known what sort of woman he expected to find waiting for him in the Charlotte, North Carolina, airport, but he recognized Rose Shepherd instantly. She stood out from among the dozens of women in the passenger walkway beyond the arrival gate. Not that she was prettier, although she was that. But there was something about the way she almost casually seemed to be aware of her surroundings, too aware. It was a look he'd first seen when he'd first gotten involved in gun smuggling as a young boy during the Spanish Civil War. It was the same look some of the men who'd gone to fight against the Fascists had in their eyes, a look of never quite being at ease, never quite feeling safe. Tom Ashbrooke had seen the look again during World War II, seen it in the eyes of men who'd spent too long at the front or too long deep behind enemy lines. The look wasn't confined only to men. He'd seen it in the faces of some of the female Resistance fighters during that war and since.

So this was the woman into whose arms his son-in-law, David Holden, had fallen after Elizabeth's death. At first glance, he approved.

He approached her, his carry-on bag in his left hand, his right hand exposed, palm open, as one might approach a too-quiet dog who might suddenly snap. "Excuse me. I'm a stranger here. Is Charleston on the same time as New York?"

There was a look in her eyes as she turned toward him, her eyes gray green, very pretty eyes, very forthright eyes, the look of startlement in them not something put there with makeup or even with practice. All he'd told her was to watch for a man with gray hair who asked a stupid question, then given her the flight number and hung up.

She smiled now. "You were right. That is a stupid question. This is Charlotte, North Carolina, not Charleston, South Carolina, and the time zone is the same regardless."

All the risk was on her side. So he identified himself. "I'm Tom Ashbrooke."

"I was expecting an older man."

"You're very flattering. I wasn't expecting anyone nearly as beautiful."

"You're flattering too. I've got a car or we can walk or get a cup of coffee," she told him, smiling, her voice a soft alto.

"Walking would be good. I've just flown more hours than I want to think about and, depending on what you tell me, I may wind up flying the same distance all over again. By my age, a lot of men have digestive troubles. I don't want to push my luck."

"Let's walk then." There was a white cardigan sweater across her shoulders, heavy enough that it could have been used as a lightweight jacket. She carried no purse. As she fell in beside him, she thrust her hands down past the wrists into the slit pockets of a full blue denim skirt. The skirt reached almost to her ankles and swayed as she walked. "I'm sorry I made you fly all the way out here. But I couldn't trust telephone communications."

"You didn't make me do anything, young lady. I wanted to come. David was more than the guy who married my daughter—always was more than that to my wife and myself. He's a good man. And now you say he's in trouble."

She was staring at her feet as he looked at her. "He's—I think he's in terrible trouble if he's still alive."

She fell silent for a second as they passed three nuns who were running toward a gate. Ashbrooke looked back over his shoulder at them, saying to Rose Shepherd "You don't trust anyone, do you?"

"These days you can't afford to. The reason I picked Charlotte for our meeting was because it was within driving distance from Metro, if I pushed, but I'd only been here once before so there was less chance of anybody recognizing me. My picture—

David's picture too—is plastered all over every post office and police station around the country; airports too."

"Then perhaps we should get to your car."

She shook her head. "It should be all right. My hair was shorter in the picture they're using and it was up. Little things like that make it a lot easier for a woman to change her appearance." And she touched at the nape of her neck, her hair loosely arranged and well past her shoulders. She took his arm, hugging it to her. "Everyone'll think you're my father or my sugar daddy."

Ashbrooke felt himself smile. "I'd be more flattered with the latter, although the former's more likely. What happened?"

"They were waiting for us. Used the remaining missiles—like the ones they used to kill the Vice President and destroy that security conference—they used them as bait. A trap. David walked right into it. The last I saw him, they'd tied him to the front of a helicopter, sort of like a shield, and they took off. We couldn't stop them. David looked unconscious—or, maybe—"

Ashbrooke exhaled slowly. "How do you know he isn't—dead, I mean?"

"The room where we found his guns and another one of our people—a good man, a quiet man—the room was filled with gas. The other man was dead, his throat slit. If they were going to kill David, why take his body?"

"There might be some reasons for that," Ashbrooke said slowly. "But logic's on your side. What would they want with him?"

She took cigarettes and a lighter from her pockets and lighted one, exhaling as she spoke. "He has everything in his head. About the—" A security guard passed them, didn't look twice, but Ashbrooke could feel her tense as she coiled her arm through his again. "About us—the—"

"I know." Ashbrooke stopped walking. There was a bench and he turned toward it. "Sit down with me."

She nodded. "All right."

Ashbrooke put down his bag, let her sit first, then sat beside her. "So, suddenly he's gone and there's no place to turn but me? What about your own organization?"

"Communications aren't that easy for us sometimes. But most of our cells have been alerted. And with Roman Makowski as President, the FBI can't help us at all. It seemed to make sense that from what David told me about you, maybe you'd have some contacts that could help. I don't know." She went to flick ashes from her cigarette, but too late, the white powdery cylinder of ash at its tip disintegrating across her blue skirt. She brushed it from her lap then stubbed out the cigarette in the ashtray beside the end of the bench.

"I know a man who might have a pipeline into your adversaries. And of course I'll help. He's in Berlin. I'll have to fly there. Whatever I find out, I'll pursue. If there's no safe means of contacting each other, you'll just have to accept it on faith that I'm doing everything possible. You can call my wife, use the same procedure you and I used on the phone when you called. I'll be calling in to her regularly, so she can keep you updated. There's a code she and I have used in the past."

Ashbrooke reached into the breast pocket of his leather jacket, extracted his wallet, shuffled through an assortment of business cards, and handed her one. She looked at it, puzzled. "It's a very simple code, using numbers and letters. Anyone worth his salt could crack it on a computer in minutes. But it sounds innocuous enough if you use it properly that no one should suspect it is a code."

"I think I understand," she said, still studying the card.

"Good. Now—tell me everything you can about the opposition."

Rose Shepherd licked her lips, looked almost casually over her shoulder, saying "Can we walk some more?"

"Sure."

They stood, Ashbrooke catching up his bag, Rose Shepherd pocketing the card. "The leader of the— of the people around Metro is a man by the name of Borsoi, Dimitri Borsoi. He uses the alias Mr. Johnson—no first name. We thought he was dead. He isn't, obviously. He works with street gangs, like the Leopards, for example, and he seems more like some kind of regional commander than the number-one big shot. But who knows?"

"Borsoi, huh—what else?"

"He's very good. I mean, he speaks perfect English, just like an American—"

Ashbrooke laughed. "I don't mean to interrupt, but if you travel as much as I do, you'll realize that what you just said is a logical contradiction. Some Americans speak the best English there is, but perfect—that would be something that would stick out like a sore thumb."

"Well, you know what I mean. He's just so normal sounding? You know?"

"What's he look like?"

"He's tall, kind of brown hair. Here—I wrote it all down." She drew a folded piece of paper from one of her pockets. Ashbrooke was beginning to wonder if her pockets were like a magician's top hat. "Eye color, everything's there." Ashbrooke didn't look at the piece of paper, simply slipped it into his pocket. "He's one of those guys," she said suddenly, "who enjoys hurting people. I guess if he's got David, he'd—I don't—" Her voice broke.

Tom Ashbrooke put his arm around the young woman's shoulders. "We'll find your David," he told her with more confidence than he felt. And she looked at him suddenly and, with tears in her eyes, she forced a smile.

They kept walking.

CHAPTER THREE

It was nearly dawn. They were coming.

They drove right into the yard between the barn and the house, two vans, four men climbing out of one, two men and a woman climbing out of the other. All of them were bristling with weaponry.

Geoffrey Kearney felt Harriet tense beside him. "Relax," he whispered.

Two of the men went around behind the house, one of those two carrying two wine bottles with rags hanging out the tops. "What are they doing?" Harriet whispered in his ear.

"Molotov cocktails. They're planning to burn down your house, remember? But we won't let them do that, Harriet. Stay here." There was a back way out of the barn and Geoffrey Kearney was up, running across the barn floor toward it, past the Jeep

Harriet's dead husband had driven there. His body was behind the wheel now. That had been hard, not only getting Harriet to help but because she refused to show any emotion and handled the dead man she'd presumably once been in love with as if he were a side of beef, and the beef was slightly rotten.

Behind him, he heard a woman's voice coming over a public address system from one of the vans. "Yo, bitch! You in the house! We're gonna burn the damn place down around your fuckin' ears. Try runnin' for it and we'll kneecap you and just throw you back inside to burn anyway. This is the justice of the people. . . ."

Kearney didn't bother listening to the rest, merely hoped she was a long-winded speaker. He was out of the barn, into the gray light now, running along the rear of the structure, the CAR-15 slung behind his back and the Smith & Wesson 9mm in his right fist.

Kearney reached the side of the barn, looked around the corner, then ran forward along its length toward the far side of the yard. He'd have to cross the yard in the open. But he'd checked the distance versus time and the ratio was pretty good. As long as the woman kept speaking, or if she stopped and the fire was set, all eyes should be in the other direction anyway. He wanted to save the house, but eliminating these cretans was his primary concern.

Kearney reached the front of the barn. The obnoxious-sounding woman was still into Karl Marx 101. Kearney licked his lips, shifting the 5904 to his left hand, grabbing the CAR-15 and shifting it forward on its sling, ready to fire it from the hip if needed. A thirty-round magazine was up the magazine well, a loose 5.56mm ball round was loaded in the chamber.

Kearney broke from concealment, running along the far side of the yard, past the silo, past the storage shed, into the small apple orchard to the side of the house. He dropped to a crouch there, checking his back. Evidently he hadn't been seen.

Kearney moved again, running along the length of the orchard for as long as he could, covering half the distance of the rear of the farmhouse. He broke toward the side of the house, the kitchen lights still visible in the gradually brightening gray of the morning.

Kearney slowed his pace as he neared the small screened-in back porch.

The two men with the Molotov cocktails were waiting patiently for the speech to end, it seemed. Their gasoline-filled wine bottles were set against the back porch steps. They stood several feet back from these, weapons slung casually at their sides, one of them smoking a cigarette. The one smoking looked to be about thirty or so, the second man a bit younger. Kearney's eyes traveled to the weapons. M-16s or AR-15s—he couldn't tell at the distance—and then, of course, each of them had a handgun or two as well.

In Kearney's own country, of course, firearms of any sort were very strictly regulated, particularly handguns. It was a policy Kearney had always considered foolishly simplistic. From all the data he had studied before setting out on this assignment, it seemed that if the people of the United States hadn't had the right to keep and bear arms—severely restricted since the troubles with the FLNA began—the country would have succumbed more easily to the FLNA onslaught. People had a basic right to defend their own lives and the lives of loved ones or innocents. Any law contravening that right was misconceived and morally unenforceable.

If Harriet was a Patriot member, these FLNA weapons (from the reports, usually stolen from police or military arsenals or illegally smuggled into the country) might serve a better purpose in better hands.

The speech, fortunately only barely audible, seemed to be winding down into redundancies. Kearney slipped the sling for his CAR-15 over his head as he reset the safety, then placed the weapon on top of the bench-type seat attached to the small picnic table behind which he'd hidden. If there had been only one man, he would have risked using a knife.

The 5904 in his right fist, the right fist pressured against his left, Kearney started toward them. The best way would be without shooting at all, and the way their weapons were positioned, if they had any brains at all, they'd give up quietly. But Geoffrey Kearney doubted they had any brains, or else they wouldn't have been there.

He crept forward, almost exactly between them, and at approximately ten yards from their backs decided to stop pushing his luck. "Neither of you move or I use my gun!" It wasn't the most original line in the world, of course, but so much of the effectiveness of any stringing together of words was in the delivery.

Both men started to turn inward, reaching for their assault rifles almost simultaneously, the one who'd been smoking snapping his cigarette butt into the pines just back from the porch. Kearney swung his body slightly left, never moving his arms, the pistol already at eye level. A double tap to the man who hadn't been smoking. Since both wore their rifles slung beside the right hip and the two men were turning toward each other, the one on the left would have less distance to traverse before he could fire, so he had to be taken out first.

Kearney arced his body right. Another double tap, through the left arm and into the left side of the neck of the smoker. Kearney swung left again, a double tap to the first man, who was already crumpling and going down. But Kearney was not certain he was dead or totally incapacitated. Kearney rectified that. He swung right again. The second man was clearly dead, the neck shot or penetration through the arm and into the heart. No time for an autopsy.

Kearney used the Smith & Wesson's safety to drop the hammer, then raised the safety again as he thrust the pistol into the right hip pocket of his black jeans. His right hand swept forward to the ballistic nylon sheath at his belt, unpouching the B&D Fazendeiro, pinching the blade between thumb and second and third fingers, levering it open. With one slice he had the sling of the nearest dead man's assault rifle cut away and was sliding the safety on and pitching it into the brush. He sliced through the second rifle's sling, grabbed up the weapon in his left hand, his left thumb feeling the safety tumbler on the left side of the frame as he shifted the tumbler confirming his suspicion that it, like the first weapon, was a full-auto-capable M-16. He closed the Fazendeiro one-handedly; no time for the sheath, he just dropped it into a pocket. Kearney racked the M-16's bolt, arcing a live round into the air past his face. Wasting it was the only way to verify that the chamber was loaded.

Kearney shifted the M-16 to his right hand, under the crook of his arm, and caught up both Molotovs by the bottle necks. He ran forward along the side of the house as he switched hands on the Molotovs, pulling his lighter from the left side pocket of his pants.

There were shouts from the front of the house. Kearney put the Zippo into his teeth, biting down on it, tasting the brass, murmuring "Yuck" under his breath. The Molotovs went back into his left hand. His right fist closed on the pistol grip of the M-16.

Two of the men who had stayed by the vans while the woman FLNA leader had proselytized were now running across the yard and toward the house. Kearney was counting on Harriet and her cowboy-style Winchester. She didn't disappoint him.

Gunfire came from the barn. The windshield of one of the vans took a hit, part of it shattering out. Kearney hugged the side of the house, resting the M-16 there, taking the solid-brass Zippo from his teeth, he held both wine bottles in his left hand. He held them near the base now, a good stretch for his hand but not impossible. He flicked back the cowling on the lighter, rolled the striking wheel under his right thumb, and ignited both Molotov cocktails.

He stuffed the lighter into his pocket, then he grabbed up the M-16 in his other hand, running. Two of the men and the woman in the yard were sheltered behind the vans, the third man was getting one of them started. Kearney threw the flaming Molotovs simultaneously, one of them smashing against the side of one of the vans, the second exploding between them. Flames. The man nearest to the Molotov that had struck the van was on fire. Kearney swung the pistol grip of the M-16 into his right hand and fired.

The burning man went down dead, spinning back into the flames.

Kearney brought the M-16 to his shoulder, firing again. The second man turned to shoot at him but never had the time.

The van that wasn't struck by the Molotov started pulling away, the woman running along beside it. She started to jump for the open side door.

There was no time to worry about her. Kearney fired for the windshield and the man behind it instead. His first burst seemed to do nothing more than glance off the windshield. There was the crack of the .30–30 from the barn, then again and again. Kearney saw Harriet standing in the barn door. The van swerved.

Kearney fired again. The windshield shattered, glass spraying laterally away from the impacts. The van crashed into the side of the barn. Kearney ran toward it, getting the 5904 out of his belt and into his left hand.

The driver of the van, face covered in blood, was spilling out the right side passenger door. Harriet's .30–30 cracked again and the man's head snapped back and he fell like a stone.

The woman. There was the stutter of a submachine gun. Kearney shouted, "Harriet! Down!"

He heard the crack of Harriet's .30–30. Then a long burst from the submachine gun.

Kearney stabbed both the M-16 and the 9mm pistol toward the FLNA woman, firing into her as the submachine gun sprayed out, her body twisting and almost dancing, crumpling like a discarded doll against the side of the van.

The M-16 was empty. Kearney threw it down. Shifting the Smith & Wesson from left to right hand, Kearney reached to the double magazine pouch on the left side of his belt, grabbing one of the two twenty-round spares there. He made a tactical magazine change as he ran, ramming the twenty into the well—it hung out at the base of the pistol's butt—and stuffing the nearly spent fourteen-rounder into his jeans pocket.

He skidded onto his knees beside the barn door. Harriet knelt there too, her head lolling forward, chin against her chest, and the rifle clutched in both hands over her thighs.

"Harriet?" He touched gently at her face with his fingertips. "Harriet?"

She raised her head and he could see the blood that covered her chest. She smiled. "What's your real name?"

"Geoff," Kearney answered softly.

"Geoff. Thank you."

She closed her eyes and died as he folded his arms around her.

CHAPTER FOUR

Mists rolled off the surface of the river in huge, cold drafts as David Holden swung down out of the saddle, catching the reins of Maria's horse in his hand. She was almost falling out of the saddle. As she slipped, he caught her, easing her to the ground, cradling her in his arms. She shivered beneath the bloodstained coat but the temperature she had seemed to run when they'd first taken to the horses had subsided, her cheeks and forehead cool but not excessively so. But it was obvious she was still very weak.

"David—you should leave me."

"I'll tell you the same thing I said the last time you told me that—nuts. You feel like your fever's down."

"*Sí—*"

"If you can stay on your horse long enough, we can get upriver from the road. Then we can rest. You'll feel better with some rest. And they won't be looking for us upriver. Maybe we can find a boat or something, trade one of the rifles for it or steal it. Or the horses. Trade those. We've got a lot of possibilities. With a boat, we can get far enough away from here that they'll never find us." He was being vastly overoptimistic, David Holden knew, but right now she needed encouragement, needed the will to go on.

"I will try. But you must promise, *si no es possible* —if it is not possible for me to go with you, you promise that you will leave me."

"It'll be possible. You picked up a mild concussion. Banged your brains around." Holden smiled. "Anybody would have reacted like you did. You need rest, that's all. Now, can I get you up on that horse again?"

Maria tried to smile.

The only travel arrangements he'd been able to make that would get him back to Europe fast enough had been through New York City to Toronto and then straight to Berlin.

He'd disembarked the aircraft at La Guardia, stretched his legs, bought a cup of coffee, then reboarded.

The sun was almost fully up now. There was a good view of the water as the aircraft started down the runway. Thomas Ashbrooke had always liked

something about La Guardia. It was smaller, certainly, than Kennedy. And there was always the water—if something went wrong with a takeoff or
landing, the water would be waiting to reach out
and grab an aircraft. It wasn't that La Guardia was
easier if you wanted in and out of midtown Manhat-
tan quickly. Maybe it all boiled down to it being less
modern.

From a slower era.

Rose Shepherd. She was very pretty, seemed gen-
uinely to love David. He didn't begrudge David
that, simply because their Elizabeth and Elizabeth
and David's children were all dead. His eyes suddenly felt hard and he looked out at the water, at
the skyline. Sometimes, at night, New York looked
so pretty.

In the daylight, few places looked pretty. The
dirt, the meanness, all the things the night hid and
the night bred were out in force and waiting to
repell the senses. He closed his eyes. And he could
see Elizabeth's face, not in life but as his daughter
had looked in her casket.

In a little while, a cabin attendant would come by
and offer him a drink. He'd take it.

Geoffrey Kearney left her there on the sofa, near
her father's trophies in her father's great room. The
other dead were where they'd fallen, except for the
man named Tom who had been her husband until
he'd joined the Front for the Liberation of North

America. Tom was where they'd put his body, behind the wheel of his Jeep inside the barn.

There was almost nothing from the FLNA killers he wanted or needed. He'd done a perfunctory search of their effects, found a notebook with some impossible-to-read scribblings inside. He'd post that to London via Toronto his first opportunity. But there was also a business card for a tavern near the lower end of the state in Milwaukee. Perhaps it was a lead to the FLNA people there, perhaps it was nothing. He was driving south anyway, though.

As he stood beside the Ford, just watching the house for a moment, he silently wished that whoever found the dead there would be with the Patriots or, at least, some friend of Harriet's or her father's. Decent burial, all of that.

He exhaled, shifted his pistol a little, and slipped behind the wheel of the car.

Kearney watched the house a moment longer. "Harriet. Thank you," he whispered.

Then he threw the automatic transmission—he hated automatic transmissions—into drive and drove out of the yard.

Rose Shepherd had pulled over at the truck stop because she was tired, not just sleepy or tired of driving. She was tired. Sleeping without David beside her was not restful. What she had never thought would happen to her had happened. She was so in love that her own life was empty when she was alone, without the one she loved.

And that could be forever.

What could Thomas Ashbrooke do? He was certainly a fine specimen of a man for his age, because his age wasn't all that obvious at all. And, according to David, Thomas Ashbrooke was well connected, very rich. What she knew of Thomas Ashbrooke she knew from the letter David had shown her that was included with the money and the gun Ashbrooke had left behind. David had found it in a safe deposit box after Elizabeth's death.

It sounded like something out of a racy novel.

But could he really find David?

If he couldn't— She lighted a cigarette, the package more full than it usually would have been. David was an infrequent smoker, sometimes going for days without lighting up. But when he did smoke, he would usually snitch one from her pack. It had become a running joke with them. She was staring at the cigarettes.

There were tears in her eyes and—as if she had a choice—Rose Shepherd just let them come. "You lousy bastards," she whispered, her throat tight, the words just making the tears come harder. "You lousy damn rotten bastards. Well—" And she blew her nose, the tears coming harder. "You think you got us, huh? 'Cause you got David? Well, fuck off and die."

There were FLNA targets to hit, and until David got back, she'd hit them, hard.

Until then.

CHAPTER FIVE

The helicopter looked like a Bell Long Ranger, and it flew low over the high canopy of trees. David Holden stood beneath the tree looking at it. Maria was in the cave about a quarter mile away, every coat and blanket with her. She'd consumed the candy bar he'd found on one of the dead men and two of the acetaminophen tablets from inside the hollow handle of his knife as well.

His stomach felt better. Empty, but better.

The sun was climbing and it was almost comfortable with the shirt on, just a little cool. The day would be warm, he knew.

There was little time for Maria to recuperate. Contrary to what he'd told her, contrary to what he himself believed, the search was concentrated seemingly just as heavily upriver as down. The leg

wound he'd given Innocentio Hernandez had probably been treated by now, and both he and Ortega de
Vasquez would be personally supervising the search
process.

If Holden and Maria stayed in one place too long,
they would be discovered. That was inevitable. If
they moved on, the chance of discovery went up,
but the certainty of it went slightly down.

He had gone out searching for food, too tired to
sleep. There had been several patches of red berries,
but the nearer to the equator, the greater the certainty that anything red growing wild was poison-
ous. He would find something. If not, he'd catch
something. Traps took time, but until Maria could
move there was no choice but to stay there, lest she
die. The cardinal rule for anyone who had sustained
a concussion was to remain as still as possible. He
had trekked her along mountain game trails, ridden
her on horseback through the end of the night and
half the morning, subjected her to temperature ex-
tremes, deprived her of rest. If he didn't wait with
her now, he could kill her. He didn't want that on
his conscience.

Holden saw a likely branch on a young tree that
was easily reached. He would have left his knife on
the ground so he couldn't fall on it, but he would
need it for the branch. Holden began shinnying up
the trunk. He remembered how his son, Dave, used
to climb so easily.

Holden closed his eyes, opened them, went on.
With some difficulty and more huffing and puffing

than he wanted to think about, he reached the branch. It was impossible for a grown man to have the energy or endurance Dave had. Holden steadied himself as best he could and took out the Crain Defender knife. For once he almost wished it was one of those survival knives with sawteeth. But it wasn't, so he chopped with the primary edge, the knife strong and sharp. After a few good swipes the branch fell away to the ground below.

Earlier, once Maria was safely ensconced, Holden fabricated a crude sheath for his knife out of several thicknesses of blanket. He doubted the sheath would do much to protect him if he fell on the Defender wrong, but it had to be better than nothing. So he resheathed the knife and started down out of the tree. He could make a bow out of the branch, and it was long enough that he could get some good action. Arrows could be made from stouter twigs to be found almost everywhere beneath the tree cover. He could risk a small fire inside the cave, to boil water for Maria and him to drink and to harden the points of the arrow shafts. The fishing line inside the hollow handle of the knife would serve as a bow-string if needed, but a better string might be made of vine if he could find the proper kind.

A gunshot might alert those who searched for them, bring them to their target. But with a bow— Holden smiled at himself as he leaned against the tree, catching his breath, the abdominal pain not nearly so bad as he had thought it would be. Whether he netted any small game with the bow or not, making it would give him something to do, to keep his mind off the slender chances he and the woman had to survive this thing.

He stuffed his hands into his pockets. The garrote he'd made of dental floss but never had to use was still there. If he was careful with the size of the bow, he already had the perfect string.

David Holden laughed at himself. If he had to stay near the cave for long while he awaited Maria's recovery, he might even build a cabin. "Yeah—I'll build a cabin. And after I'm through with that, I can build a dormer as an addition. Yeah! Hey—why not build a boat? A yacht? I could build a giant hang glider and Maria and I could go back up to the highest mountain peak we could find and jump off and soar all the way back home. So long, Peru! Hello, Metro! And then—" Holden doubled over with laughter, wondering on one level of consciousness if he'd gone crazy.

The sound of the helicopter—it was very close—made him stop laughing.

CHAPTER SIX

A voice he could hardly understand over the murmuring crowd was issuing information about boarding calls for unintelligible flight numbers. He cut across the two lanes of pedestrian traffic on the E concourse and made it safely to the wall and a drinking fountain. He was thirsty. He told himself that he was thirsty because it was suddenly so hot, getting off the plane from Metro and into the terminal. But he realized it was probably because he was overdoing things a little. Out of the hospital one day, quick reservations for Chicago, and gone the next morning. All the others were gone, home to their families or off on other assignments, the busywork kind of assignments that were designed to punish an agent. But none of them was still in Metro.

It was odd. For the first time in his life since high school, Luther Steel was without a job. Of course, he still had a paycheck, but for how long he didn't know. And they wouldn't fire him, just ask him to resign, make it clear that he must. So, getting another job in law enforcement wouldn't be difficult. These days, skilled law enforcement professionals were needed everywhere to combat the menace of the FLNA, and being black didn't make a bit of difference. There was always private security work. Security people were making a fortune; every home and business that could afford it were hiring more protection than overworked police personnel could provide.

But the Federal Bureau of Investigation was as much a part of his life as his wife and his children. He looked into the mirror each morning when he shaved and saw Luther Steel, Special Agent.

As he looked into the darkened glass over the rent-a-car advertisement, Steel saw another face, the skin like his own. The face was somehow better looking. Craggy, smiling, chiseled from stone but by an artist with a sense of humor. "Didn't Rudy tell you somebody'd be meeting you at the airport?"

Rudy—Rudolph Cerillia, FBI director in Coventry since the President had been so seriously injured and gone into a coma from which the experts said there was almost no chance of recovery.

Luther Steel turned around slowly.

The blue eyes, the graying black hair, the black

leather jacket, the collar snapped up so cool. "Mr. Saddler—I didn't realize he meant you, sir."

"I told you, boy—Rocky."

"Yes, sir—Rocky." Rocky Saddler's age—aside from the fact that it had to be considerably advanced—didn't show. It just didn't show. And the man amazed Luther Steel. He extended his right hand. "Rocky—it's so good to see you, sir."

"Understand you're in deep shit, Steel."

Luther Steel looked away and shrugged his shoulders, then looked back and shrugged again. "Yes, I guess you could say that. The acting director will probably get around to asking for my resignation as soon as he thinks I'm well enough."

"You look pretty fit to me."

"I got banged up a little when the missile hit the presidential helicopter up there on the roof of the phone company building. But I'm in pretty good shape now. How's your daughter, sir?"

"Fine. I'm fine too. Now that we're through with that shit, let's get moving."

"You're going to—"

"I've driven to Wisconsin before. Trust me; I know the way. I bet you're anxious."

"To see my wife and children? Yes, sir." Luther Steel nodded, reaching for his two pieces of carry-on luggage. But Rocky Saddler already had them. "Look—I'll take—"

"I've got them." Rocky Saddler started off into the crowd and Steel realized he'd better stop staring after him and start keeping up with him.

* * *

Geoffrey Kearney sat at the counter and sipped his coffee. In the mirror behind the counter, he could see everyone who came into or out of the truck stop. And, at the counter, he could hear talk about what was going on down the road. The talk confirmed the CB transmissions he'd intercepted throughout the morning. There were roving groups of police cars working the roads in some sort of apparently random search pattern, stopping every motorist, trucker or otherwise, searching cars top to bottom, checking driver's licenses, insurance papers, asking questions about where people were going and why. At the slightest provocation, they would conduct detailed searches, including frisks. They were looking for the Patriot band that had allegedly caused the deaths of nine people on a farm just south of Lake Superior. The waitress brought his hot roast beef sandwich. The open-faced sandwich and the mashed potatoes were drowning in dark-brown gravy, but the meal looked oddly appetizing. He supposed hunger made the difference. It even smelled good.

Kearney ate ravenously, into a third cup of black coffee and a piece of apple pie before he felt sated. He lighted a cigarette, eavesdropping on the interesting conversation of the truckers in the booth immediately behind him.

". . . asked the cop what happened to that 'probable cause' stuff, right?"

"And what'd he say?"

"Tells me I keep shootin' my mouth off, he'll bust me for suspicion. I tell ya, Deke, what the hell kinda country is this becomin'?"

"I don't think no Patriots iced them nine people on that farm. FLNA bastards. That's who it was. Or maybe no nine people was killed at all, huh? Maybe they're usin' this as some kinda excuse to start restrictin' travel. It'll come. I heard that one of Makowski's top-priority bills in Congress is gonna be a law to issue national ID cards. The news was talkin' about it last night. Says it'll make it harder for the FLNA and the Patriots to travel around. Make it more easy to arrest 'em. He's full o' shit. That's what I think."

Kearney doubted the trucker would get many cogent arguments to the contrary. Makowski, at least, seemed full of that mythic substance. Yet it almost seemed there was a method to his attempts to instantly modify the nation. The call for a complete ban on private firearms ownership except certain target pistols to be determined suitable for civilian sporting use by the Treasury Department in consultation with a review board, the ban specifically directed at semiautomatic pistols in calibers larger than .22 Long Rifle or with magazine capacity greater than ten rounds, and all semiautomatic long guns, both rifles and shotguns. Makowski was calling the events that had brought him into the White House a national tragedy of unparalleled proportions. At least, Kearney thought, smiling, the chap was right about that.

The talk stopped and Kearney looked up from his
coffee. Four police officers entered through the front
door, and from the corridor along which the bath-
rooms were located (there was a back door at the
end of that corridor) two more police officers entered. Two of them carried World War II vintage
M1 Carbines. A couple of the truckers stood up. A
waitress somewhere off to Kearney's left dropped a
tray of dirty dishes. She just stood there, beside the
mess on the floor, staring.

One of the police officers, a florid-faced man of
about fifty, cleared his throat and announced, "We
have reason to believe that the murderer or murderers of those nine people might be in this immediate
vicinity. Sorry to inconvenience you folks, but we're
gonna run a weapons check and check IDs. If
you're innocent, you got nothin' to worry about. If
you aren't, may as well give up now. There's more
of us outside so you can't get away."

Suddenly Kearney remembered something the female FLNA leader had said during her speech before the firebombing was to begin. He had been so
absorbed in his own business of taking out the two
men at the rear of the house that he'd totally missed
the significance of her words. He sipped at his coffee, watching the tableau of police searches in the
mirror as it began unfolding behind him. The
woman had said something about both Harriet and
"Tommy" dying. At the time, Kearney hadn't
thought twice about it, thinking she meant Tom,
Harriet's husband, FLNA revenge and all that on

someone who'd broken discipline. But Tommy could have meant something else. Like "Limey" or "Brit," it could have meant him.

Geoffrey Kearney stubbed out his cigarette. It was becoming increasingly apparent to him that someone on the Canadian end, or perhaps even in London, was a pipeline to the FLNA. If the police came for him, he'd know for certain that his identity was blown. If they didn't, he'd know simply that limited information had been put out, that his identity was unknown. First, there was the attack that had killed Harriet's father, the Patriot coordinator he was to have worked with, then the attack on the farmhouse. More than coincidence? Was the "Tommy" thing just paranoia from too many years in the business?

"How about you? Stand up, please."

Kearney looked in the mirror and smiled across his coffee cup. With his best American accent, the one he'd been using since he'd entered the truck stop, he said, "Who—me?"

"Yeah, you."

Kearney stood up.

"Put your hands out on the counter and step back from them, lean."

The policeman was a head shorter than he. Kearney inclined his head downward and looked the man in the eye. The safety on the M1 Carbine held by the nearest of the two officers was still set to on. It would have been easy enough to make a break for it. He put his hands on the counter, then started stepping back, leaning, but not quite enough so it wouldn't appear that he'd done it before. "I got my rights. Where the hell's the warrant, man?"

"Keep talkin' like that, you'll see a warrant damn quick, pal. Farther back—really lean on 'em!"

Kearney obliged. He was totally without obvious weapons. But the manner in which the police officer —it was probably his hundredth frisk of the day— conducted the patdown was such that, had Kearney been carrying in the small of the back or had a diminutive pistol such as a .25 automatic in a crotch holster or something, it would never have been found.

The patdown was over.

"Let's see some ID, sir."

Kearney slowly moved his feet toward the counter and reached under his coat, the muscles around the police officer's eyes visibly tensing. Kearney tossed his wallet down on the counter.

"Let's see your driver's license."

Kearney was running with the Texas driver's license at the moment, matching the Texas plates on the car. The concealed weapons permits, the other driver's licenses were stored inside the hidden compartments of the car along with his weapons. "Texan, huh?"

"I live there. I wasn't born there."

"Where were you born—" And the policeman looked at the license again. "—Mr. Hawthorne?"

"Chicago."

"I've been to Chicago—"

"Yeah—me too."

"What part of Chicago you from?"

"Southside—there's another part?"

The cop laughed. "What's your business up here?"

"Had some time off, so I came up to see my old place, see some places I haven't seen since I was a kid."

"Travelin' alone?"

"Yeah."

"What do you do for a living?"

"I'm a securities analyst," Kearney lied.

"Security guards and stuff?"

"No—stocks and bonds and stuff."

"Right. Let's see some corroborating ID."

Kearney took out the American Express card with the name William Hawthorne on it, a Visa card with the same name, a gasoline credit card with the same name. "Good enough?"

"Where's the registration and proof of insurance on the car?"

"In the glove compartment."

"Your car?"

"Yeah. My car."

"In the glove compartment, you say?"

"Yeah—want me to get it?"

"Don't smart off." He tossed the driver's license and the credit cards on the countertop, the driver's license landing in Kearney's plate with the remains of the piece of apple pie. Kearney just looked at him. "Thank you for your cooperation, sir. Drive carefully and have a pleasant stay here."

"You bet." Kearney nodded.

The policeman walked on a few positions down the counter to the next unfortunate and began the same routine. Women weren't being body searched, thankfully, but had to empty the contents of their purses, Kearney observed in the mirror as he sat down again. The coffee was cold. He took the William Hawthorne driver's license out of the remains of the pie and wiped it clean on a paper napkin, then replaced license and credit cards in his wallet and pocketed the wallet.

His coffee was cold. "Miss—could I have more coffee?"

"Yeah—sure." The waitress came with the customary half-filled Pyrex globe and poured. "Anything else?"

"You can take this, please." He gestured toward the plate with his pie.

She nodded and took it. He nodded his thanks. Kearney kept watching, sipping at the hot coffee. So, if there was a leak, his face wasn't known, and neither were the false identities he was using.

The policeman had been courteous enough, he supposed. But he didn't much like police searches in a supposedly free nation. In Communist Eastern Europe, in parts of Africa or Latin America or Asia, they were a matter of course. Not here. He tried reading the faces of the policemen—it didn't look as if most of them liked the idea very much either.

He'd been in the United States on several occasions over the years, sometimes just passing through, sometimes on official business, once (he'd spent three weeks touring the Southwest and loved every minute of it, almost deciding to retire to Albuquerque, New Mexico, if he lived to retire) on vacation. But when he was with the RCMP chief inspector there in Metro they both noticed—suddenly everything seemed terribly, irrevocably different in the United States.

There was fear.

Kearney sipped at his coffee.

CHAPTER SEVEN

Patsy Alfredi, Mitch Diamond, and some of the others stood around her. Rose Shepherd stabbed her hands into the pockets of her black M-65 field jacket. "If they think they pulled our plug when they put the bag on David, we're gonna show 'em they thought wrong. There's that FLNA garage we've been talkin' about hitting—"

"Hey, Rosie," Patsy interrupted.

"Yeah?"

"Didn't we put off tryin' to do somethin' about that place because the numbers kept changing all the time? Sometimes only a half-dozen FLNAers there, sometimes five or six times that many?"

"Would you have followed David there?" It was an unfair question to ask and she knew it, but she asked it anyway.

Patsy licked her lips. "So, when do we move out?"

Rose Shepherd looked at her wristwatch. "An hour. We want to hit 'em just before dinner, and it'll take us an hour to get there. We ran the plan over a dozen times, but we'll do it again. Get all the troops and meet me by the storage house in ten minutes." Without another word, she turned on her heel and walked back toward the small tent she had shared with David.

It was the thing with her eyes and her throat again, the tightness. She sniffed, pulling back the tent flap, passing inside, pulling the flap closed behind her. She needed sleep. But she needed to do something even more, to strike back at the FLNA.

She took David's Desert Eagle from the suitcase he used like a dresser and dropped to her knees on the ground cloth that was the floor of the tent. It was hard to see in the tent, but that was good. She didn't want to see a lot of things—like his combat boots or the T-shirt he sometimes wore that she kept telling herself it would be wrong to sleep in.

The Desert Eagle .44 was a heavy gun, but when she held it as if she were about to shoot it, it balanced well in her hand. The reach was a little long for her, but she could make it to the trigger if she twisted her hand around a little. Rufus had let her shoot it a few times. So had David.

The Desert Eagle had been Rufus Burroughs's gun. After that thing in Ralph Kaminsky's office where the Metro deputy commander had tried bust-ing the best cop in the world—Rufus had been the best—because he was trying to fight the bad guys, she and Rufus had escaped, gone into hiding like so many Patriots before and since. Rufus had never been without the .44 Magnum automatic.

And then there was the raid on Plant Wright when the FLNA had been about to cause a core meltdown. Rufus and David together had stopped the FLNA cold, but Rufus died of the wounds he sustained there.

David took the pistol to use as his own. Rose Shepherd had always known why: a badge of leadership and a constant reminder of the man who'd used it with such honor.

Rose Shepherd stood up in the center of the tent. She picked up the black Southwind Sanctions SAS holster for the pistol. It was easily adjustable.

She set down the pistol and shrugged off her coat, feeling a little cold. She threaded the drop shank under her BDU pants belt and closed the buckle on the shank, securing it. Then she began to shorten the length of the shank.

She checked the pistol—unloaded—and positioned it in the holster so the holster would hang right. She adjusted the shank a little more, then began to shorten the two straps that would secure the holster at her right thigh.

Finished, the straps closed, she checked the spare magazine pouch. The magazine had eight rounds loaded. After replacing the magazine in the pouch and securing the safety strap over it, she picked up

the gun and dropped to her knees beside the suitcase.

She reached for a red and white box, filled with
Federal 180-grain Jacketed Hollow Points. She buttoned out the magazine and began loading it, slipping each round carefully under the feed lips. Finally loaded, she placed the magazine up the
magazine well. It was hard to hold the gun and
work the slide with hands her size, but retracting
the slide wasn't as difficult as she'd remembered it
being. With a round in the chamber, she carefully
controlled the hammer as she worked the trigger,
lowering the hammer over the chambered round.

Still on her knees, she eased the pistol into the
black ballistic holster at her right thigh and closed
the safety strap.

She licked her lips.

The ten minutes had to be up.

Time for the meeting by the storage building to
go over the plan.

She stood up.

"David."

CHAPTER EIGHT

David Holden virtually incinerated the rabbit he'd taken with his improvised bow. It was an old habit that if he hunted rabbit, which he hadn't done in years, he'd always hunt after the first frost. If he hunted before a first frost, he'd been taught by his father to deep freeze the rabbit before eating. Whether the first frost or the deep freezing had the desired effect of eliminating parasite infestation, he had no way of knowing. But he'd never gotten sick from rabbit.

With no first frost and certainly no deep freeze available, he did the next best thing, overcooking.

"That smells good."

"It tastes pretty much like chicken; or at least rabbits do where I come from. You look better, Maria."

"My head—it still hurts, but not very much. I feel better. I should cook for you. You hunted, you brought the wood for the fire—"

"I'm sorry about the smoke." He had been fanning the smoke from the fire farther toward the rear of the cave, both to avoid smoking out Maria and to dissipate the smoke before it eventually exited the cave. He had checked the cave thoroughly when they entered. It dead-ended totally some fifty yards back, and there was no evidence of bat droppings.

"You are a good doctor," she told him.

He laughed at that. His doctorate was a Ph.D. in history; the only medical training he had was that given to all special warfare personnel, and that was back in his SEAL Team days. Years before any of this.

"You're too kind. With a good rest tonight and a good meal, we can take the horses tomorrow and try to make it to that boat I was talking about," Holden told her. "And if you don't feel quite up to it, no problem—we'll wait until you do. No evidence at all that they're looking for us in this direction," he lied. But the lie was necessary. He needed her to give an honest evaluation of her health before they tried making it out again. It would be to no one's advantage if she lied in order to be accommodating and a few hours later could not go on without risk to her life. "Hope you like your rabbit well done."

"I am hungry. I will like it any way, I think, David."

He figured he'd burned it enough. Using the Defender knife to help keep from dropping it as he took the little spit he'd made off the forked sticks on which he rotated it, he transferred the rabbit to the mat of leaves he'd made earlier.

"Tell me about your woman," she said. "I am—curious? Is that the word?"

Holden looked over his shoulder at her, saying "What do you want to know about her?"

"Her name is Rosita?"

He laughed. "No—Rosie. It's really Rose, and I think she was ticked with me when I first—"

"Tick-ed?"

"Ticked. Irritated. Upset. I don't think she liked it when I started calling her Rosie, but she does now. She was a cop."

"A policeman?"

"Policewoman, actually. Yeah. A detective. She's better with a gun than most men and she's a tough fighter. She's very beautiful."

"You love her very much, David. I can tell from your voice, from the way you say her name."

Holden stood up and brought over part of the rabbit. "Can you get yourself sitting up?"

"Sí—" Slowly—he watched her eyes and she winced a little as she moved—she sat up against the blankets and coats he'd used to make a bed for her. "Aiegh! Mucho calor!"

"Like my mother used to tell me, why would I have cooked it if it wasn't supposed to be hot?

Hmm? Take it slow." Holden moved back toward the fire to get some of the rabbit for himself. He took a bite as he came forward to join Maria and sit beside her. It tasted a little gamier than the rabbit Elizabeth occasionally bought in the supermarket, and it was definitely overcooked. But he was hungry enough that it tasted good. "You know anything about fish?"

"Ohh, *sí*—my father, when I was very little—he would take me to fishing."

"Can you eat the fish out of this river we're heading for? I mean, is the water clean enough? What kind—"

"I do not know the names, but people fish in the river all the time and they do not get sick. I know which fish by the way they look."

"Tell you what." Holden smiled. "As soon as we get the chance, why don't we do this? I'll catch 'em and you tell me which ones to throw back, okay?"

"Esta bien, David. Do you think—do—"

"That we'll make it out of here?" One of the horses whinnied. Holden set down his food. "Sure we will," he told her, standing up, grabbing the M-16 beside him, and going closer to the mouth of the cave. "Sure we will."

Overhead, he could faintly hear the sounds of a helicopter. Maria wouldn't be able to hear the sounds where she was. That was good.

David Holden's appetite was suddenly gone, but he told himself that he had to eat anyway.

* * *

Traffic had been starting to bottleneck for the last ten miles and now was at a standstill.

Luther Steel's suspicions were confirmed at last. He could see the cause of the bottleneck in the distance.

There was a police roadblock at the Illinois–Wisconsin border, officers from both state police units manning it, stopping traffic in both directions. Luther Steel looked at Rocky Saddler. "Listen—pass me your gun."

"Guns, Luther."

"Shit—guns, then. I'll say they're mine. My shield should get us through." There was a helicopter flying over the highway. Steel strained to look for police markings. But it was National Guard instead.

"That's really nice of you, Luther." And Saddler laughed. "Whenever I'm off my turf, my man, I plan around such little inconveniences. The High Power and the TEC-9 are stashed. Nobody'll find them unless they fluoroscope the car. And you can take that to the bank."

"When did these roadblocks start?"

"Same day the missile hit that meeting and the Vice President was killed. I don't know if Roman Makowski directly started it or what, but I understand a lot of the states are doing it. Sort of like trying to smuggle fruit out of California." Saddler laughed, his face seaming. "It'll pass. Or we'll pass it, either way. The roadblocks only run for an hour or two. There isn't enough manpower to do it twenty-four hours a day."

"And the helicopter?"

"Think about it."

Steel did. "Anybody who turns off to avoid the roadblock gets a car sent to cut him off, right?"

"You've got it. But you can get around it most of the time anyway. Do a little more thinking."

"They'd arrest you if they found a scanning monitor." The one mounted in Saddler's car the last time was missing now. "The scanning monitor's hidden too?"

"Just don't turn on the radio when the police start asking for our ID, that's all."

"You put an AM/FM radio front on a scanning monitor."

"A little less simple than that." Saddler nodded, lighting one of his rare cigarettes. "I had the thing built. You can still get AM and FM and play cassettes. But there's a simpler way to avoid the roadblocks than a scanning monitor. Use the CB."

"The highway police must monitor that," Steel said.

"Sure, but not the side bands. And anyway, they can't trace a signal back to its origin. You can say anything you want." Saddler grinned as he exhaled cigarette smoke. "Has it occurred to you that Roman Makowski's people might want to do more than disband the Metro Task Force?"

"What did Mr. Cerillia say?"

Saddler seemed to study the red glowing tip of his

cigarette. "He just echoed my own worries for you and the others. Think about it for a minute. Makowski has essentially pulled Rudy's plug, right? But he wants it to stay pulled. If you guys are alive, especially you, you can corroborate anything Rudolph Cerillia says about the President giving him direct orders to run the squad."

"How did you know that?"

Saddler smiled his smile again. "Didn't take a genius to figure that out after Rudy called me and asked me to help that first time. When I learned he'd been booted out of his job for all intents and purposes, a presidential directive seemed a forgone conclusion. But what if you were dead? What if they could blame your death on the Patriots? Make it look like some sort of internecine violence? They'd have your boss and my friend by the short hairs. And who'd be able to stop them? When the President finally dies, Makowski's going to use that as his excuse to do whatever he wants in the name of making the country safe. People like you won't like that."

"What about people like you, Mr. Saddler?" Steel almost whispered.

"I'll be harder to track down. I sent my daughter up to visit some friends. She bitched like crazy about all the stuff she had to do at the university and everything, but I made her do it. No other way they can get to me except getting to me myself. If I were you, I'd take that family of yours and go deep, my man."

"What do you mean? Run?"

"They're going to try to hit you." As Saddler spoke, Steel became progressively more uncomfortable. "Don't worry about it now. They want you, not them. Your wife and children would only be a wedge to get you. And they have to do it fast, so you don't have time to blow the whistle to the newspapers or anything, assuming any newspaper these days would print the truth. They'll hit you after you've rejoined your family."

"There are Marshals Service personnel guarding them."

"The marshals are like the marines, always faithful. But how many marshals?"

Steel watched the traffic ahead of them. It was starting to crawl forward slightly. "Six. Two per shift, three shifts."

"Say they hit when all six deputy marshals are having a meeting or something, so you've got the maximum amount of protection. Say they hit you so hard it doesn't do any good how many deputies are guarding you and your family."

"You're suggesting—"

"I'm suggesting something I know you won't do, Steel. So, if you don't have any objections, I'll stay in Wisconsin awhile. Just long enough until whoever they get to kill you makes the play. With me around, you've got a damn sight better chance."

Steel just looked at him. In another man, such a remark would have been lunatic bravado. In Rocky Saddler, it was merely a statement of fact. "Thank you. But I hope you're wrong. If I thought the government—or even just a part of it—would try to murder a man and his family because of—"

"To suppress the truth, Luther, you'd be surprised what some people would do." Saddler had waited until there was approximately two hundred yards between him and the car ahead, but now started edging his car forward. Steel looked at his watch. The roadblock was taking forever. "You're a very experienced man when it comes to fighting criminals and protecting the public. When it comes to understanding the methodology of power and protecting yourself, I'm afraid you're very, very naive. It wouldn't be the government. It'd be Roman Makowski, and through so many people nobody'd ever trace it back to him no matter what happened. Men who've wanted to be dictators have wiped out whole populations when it suited their purpose. Killing some white-hatted black fed and his wife and children is next to nothing for people like that. If they take some deputy marshals out at the same time, then they do. You'll learn the hard way. And if you survive it, you'll be the better man for it. If you don't, well, you'll have died a good guy."

"You're really cheerful, Mr. Saddler. You must be great fun at a party."

Saddler opened his window and snapped out the butt of his cigarette. "Parties, funerals—whatever. Seen a lot of both in my time."

CHAPTER NINE

The Charter River ran through East Perimeter Metro like an open wound. In the days when Rose had gone down to the river with her father, sometimes the wound had festered with garbage and soapsuds. But now the river was considerably cleaner. It even smelled like water.

The first time her dad had taken her down to the river, she remembered crinkling up her nose and asking him "Daddy, what's that bad smell?"

"People don't take care of things like they should, Rosie. You never see an animal relieving itself in a watering hole. People do it. People dump everything imaginable in a river and then the next second they complain that the water's dirty."

Rose Shepherd had never thought about it before that way, but her father, in his own way, was a prophet for the era of ecology. He never lived to see it.

The warehouse that the FLNA was using as their new garage was on the other side of the bridge, located on an island about two miles square in one of the oldest industrial areas in the Metro area. Abandoned by industry decades earlier, it became a collection of derelict factories and low-rent warehouses. The bridge was a drawbridge, the kind that opened and closed to allow higher traffic than barges and speedboats through. The control kiosk for the bridge was on the side nearest the warehouse.

Because of the bridge itself and because, if the FLNA had to, the bridge could be controlled from their side, David had put off raiding the facility. "Why not hit it now?" she'd asked him more than once.

"Because you can't come up on them from their own side unless you use power boats or diving equipment. We don't have the diving equipment, power boats would be too noisy, and, if we rowed up and were spotted, shooting us would be like shooting fish in a barrel. I'm not talking a unit of SEALs here, I'm talking about some Vietnam vets, some ex-cops, some salesmen, some housewives, a hairdresser, and a garage mechanic. Okay? The only way is to get a small force across the bridge and take the bridge house, then hold it without them knowing it and when the garage starts to empty out, we open the drawbridge, trapping them in our kill zone. That's the only way. Since the number of personnel seems to vary radically almost daily, there's no telling when we should hit. If we send in enough people to handle the higher numbers, we'll be spotted for sure because the only time we can get across the bridge and take the bridge house is during daylight. At night the police and military helicopters make random sweeps along the river, and we'd run too much of a risk of being spotted."

She had settled on six Patriots, herself included. Patsy Alfredi was in charge of the residual force that would cover their retreat from the city side.

All five of the Patriots who had volunteered and been accepted were men. She would only take volunteers because of the inordinately high risk factor, but everyone at the camp had volunteered.

The men she selected all had previous military training, one of them a marine recon veteran. All had proven themselves in previous engagements. None of them was married or had children or other dependents.

She sat in the back of the van with them now. "Harry—you'll take the second squad and start across the bridge once you get the signal from the bridge kiosk that we control it."

Harry—black, about thirty-eight years old, lean to the point of looking skinny—said, "You'll start the flag over the bridge house down, then bring it partway up again, then take it down for the night."

"You got it," Rose Shepherd told him.

She turned to the two men who would go with

her across the bridge undercarriage. Like her, and unlike Harry and the men of his squad, they were dressed in the black BDUs that had become the de facto battle uniform of the Patriots. "We move out—" She looked at her watch. "We move out in two minutes. We cross the bridge and come up behind the bridge house. We have enough explosives with us to take out the bridge if we have to, but I don't want to unless that's the only way to nail these FLNAers. So Bob"—she looked at the tall, red-headed man closest to her— "you'll keep the special charges we made up for the bridge and be ready to place them. But don't unless I tell you to. If I buy it, you'll have to take Harry's judgment on it. He'll be second in command."

Bob nodded, saying "The charges are big enough; all I'll need is a couple of minutes—only three to plant. They'll rip open the hinge where their side of the bridge rises and that'll do the job. Like I said, if any of us are near it, we're gone."

"Gotchya." Rose nodded. "So—Bob, Moe. We get control of the bridge, we wait until sundown and work the flag. Harry and his guys come along and get back near the warehouse. When the FLNA guys start leaving the warehouse and we figure we've got most of them, we raise the bridge and Moe—Bob helps him—opens up with the machine gun." The M-60 was liberated from the FLNA weeks before. "Bob and Moe will keep the FLNA personnel pinned down so Harry and his men have a free shot at the warehouse while we kill as many of them as possible. Harry's team steals a car or something from the warehouse. As soon as their charges are ready to go, they signal on the radio that they're ready. We use the gas grenades against the guys on the bridge. They think we're planning to attack. But we let the bridge down. They take the chance and cross. We hope. Patsy, on this side of the bridge, gets as many of them as she can with her people. We hop in the car Harry liberates and drive like hell. Patsy'll steer the FLNA personnel still alive by then to the south. We'll escape to the north. When we hit the middle of the bridge, Harry detonates the explosives laid in the sewers under the street leading to the warehouse, to get any of the FLNA personnel who flee that way. Any questions?"

"You come up with this, Rosie?" It was Harry who asked the question.

"Why?"

"It's a lot more detailed than some of David's plans. I mean, he's tops, but you're tops too."

Rose Shepherd leaned across the open space between them and planted a kiss on him.

It was time to go. As she started from the van, she felt the added weight on her thigh. The Desert Eagle.

This one was for David, and she hoped her ego wasn't going to make it a disaster. She looked first, then jumped down onto the gravel surface of the parking lot. The lot was mere feet above the surface of the river, and during spring floods—which hadn't occurred in years—it was usually underwater. This was her home precinct and she knew it like the back of her hand, every season of the year, day and night.

She wondered if that was part of the reason why she wanted to hit this target so badly, because it was in what had been her own backyard. Or because her father had taken her down by this bridge when she was little. Or because of David.

The five men were out of the van. An M-16 in her right hand, Rose Shepherd broke into a dead run for the nearest foundation pillar. She thought the sounds of her own feet and the running feet behind her were terribly loud. She skidded to a halt beside the foundation pillar's base and, dropping into a crouch, covered the five men. Harry, at a nod from her, was the first one up into the girders, climbing at a good pace, Bob after him. Rose Shepherd fell in next, climbing as rapidly as she could, her M-16 slung behind her.

Harry had reached the first tie brace, a diagonal leading up into the main tower legs.

That was the only tricky part that required any kind of real climbing, and Harry had been a gymnast in high school and college and had a rope to get the rest of them up if needed. Once up, the service walkway spanned the bridge over the river to the other side. The catwalk was narrow but should get them across.

Bob was hanging back as she reached the tie brace, Harry already to the top and onto the catwalk, a rope snaked down. "What's the matter?"

"I'm afraid of heights. It hasn't bothered me in years, but—"

"I'm starting up that girder," Rose Shepherd told him. "And I'll be right behind you." Harry shook the rope for them to hurry along. Rose Shepherd grabbed for it, handed it to Bob. "If you fall, I'll fall too. And I'm not going to let you fall. Is that all right?"

"You're a hell of a guy," Bob said softly, forcing a smile. "I won't let you down." He started up the tie brace.

Rose Shepherd checked that the unfamiliar SAS holster carrying the .44 Desert Eagle was secure. It was. Her gloved hands grasped the rope and she started up, feeling almost silly, like Batman in the old 1960s television show, walking up the wall of a building. But the angle was an almost exact forty-five degrees and, once she had the feel of it, moving along the tie brace seemed relatively easy.

If the rope snapped, she'd fall to the rocks that formed the riverbank here, rocks that had been brought in when the island was first used as an industrial site, long before this bridge was built.

As she looked down—a mistake, she realized as she did it—she could see some of the old bridge pylons still visible in the water, a combination of natural stone and concrete. She looked away from the swirling water below and toward Bob just ahead of her. His legs were trembling visibly. But she didn't count him any less of a man for it. To conquer a fear like that obviously took more courage than to zip up the diagonally running girder like Harry had, with no thought of fear.

Bob reached the top of the tie brace, Harry helping him up onto the catwalk. Rose Shepherd kept walking. Once she inadvertently shifted her rear end back and, hence, her center of gravity. She almost lost her balance. She regained it fully and kept moving, welcoming the clasp of Harry's hands over hers as she reached the top.

She climbed onto the catwalk, looking back to the other three men, already starting to move. There was no time to watch them.

She slipped past Bob. Although she never thought of herself as small, by comparison to a full-grown man she was. Ahead of him now, the M-16 slung forward, her thumb over the safety tumbler, Rose Shepherd started out beneath the bridge span. The catwalk vibrated under her weight and she told herself it was safe, but gestured Bob to hang back so their weight would be more evenly distributed.

Ahead of her, she could see the concrete base of the bridge kiosk.

CHAPTER TEN

Maria had fallen asleep again.

He was grateful for that. David Holden took a sip of boiled water and swished it in his mouth. It still tasted odd, but logic told him it was safe to drink. Swishing the water didn't have the desired effect. His teeth still felt dirty, despite the stick he'd used to brush them and his gums.

He wasn't about to trust his gums to fishing line and the dental floss garrote that was now his bow string. Bits of rabbit flesh were stuck in his teeth. The same thing happened when he ate chicken or corn. He assumed he wasn't the only person with such a problem, but how was it that Maria—he'd seen her teeth clearly when she smiled—didn't have it? There was a sort of congenital neatness about most women, Holden thought.

He could have used a cigarette. And that, like almost everything else, made him think about Rosie. It had become a running joke between them that he was always filching cigarettes from her purse and filching her lighter to light them. What was she doing now?

He could see the sun in the distance above the high jungle's canopy. It was lowering rapidly. The speed wouldn't be as evident where Rosie was. Sunsets lingered there.

For all of the problems of just day-to-day existence in the Metro area, the constant cat and mouse with the FLNA and the police, he realized how much better off he'd been there. Once he got out onto the river, then what? Even assuming that he and Maria were able to escape the men pursuing him, how would he get out of South America? How could he reenter the United States without being discovered? How could he get to Metro and return to Rosie Shepherd?

He had avoided these questions since he'd first contemplated his escape, avoided them because there seemed to be no answer. A step at a time, he'd told himself every time one of the nagging questions surfaced at the back of his mind. There had to be smugglers, there had to be regular clandestine routes in and out of the country that law enforcement personnel were not aware of.

There had to be.

What would he do with Maria?

She had to have family somewhere. He could get her to them and they would care for her.

He began to organize his plans. If she was well enough the next morning, they would move on, taking it easy. With a river this size there would be boats. Maria probably knew the area well enough; he remembered what she'd said about going fishing. He could trade the two horses and their tack—they were good-looking animals, and well broken—and, if necessary, trade one of the M-16s and a few rounds of ammunition. He could get a boat.

With a boat, his problems wouldn't be solved, but if he waited until cover of night, they could make it past the U-shaped bend in the trail that paralleled the river, getting past most of Innocentio Hernandez's men. Once clear of the trail, the current would carry them well away from this place. To where, David Holden wasn't quite certain. His Latin American history was reasonably strong, but his Latin American geography wasn't that detailed.

But somewhere along the way the Amazon flowed into Brazil. Once he was there, he could sell off an M-16—or another one—and get enough money to try to contact— Whom would he contact?

He couldn't call Rosie on the phone. He could call Lem Parrish. But the Patriot radio personality's telephone might be tapped by the FLNA or the police. He could—David Holden exhaled, wishing again for a cigarette, thinking again of Rosie Shepherd.

The only logical person to call was Thomas Ashbrooke, his father-in-law.

Elizabeth's father.

He didn't know the number, but he knew the name of the town in Switzerland where his wife's parents had their chalet.

A chalet, for God's sake, Holden thought.

It was hard to imagine people living a lifestyle like that.

But he could call Thomas Ashbrooke. If Tom had told the truth in that letter of his that was in the safety deposit box along with the huge amount of money and the Walther P-38—and Tom Ashbrooke always told the truth, even when it hurt—then he would have the connections to find a route out of Brazil and back into the United States.

To Rosie.

To the war that seemed as if it might never end.

He'd never liked Tom Ashbrooke, but he respected him. He guessed he'd resented the money, and all the more since he'd found out where it came from in the wake of Elizabeth and the children's deaths.

But at least he had a plan.

He wished he had a cigarette.

He wished he had Rosie Shepherd.

CHAPTER ELEVEN

Geoffrey Kearney's scanning monitor, built into the dashboard and worked with the same controls used for the digital clock, tripped onto a frequency on which there had been no traffic before.

"This is Forager calling Constellation. The last guest has arrived. I say again, the last guest has arrived. Over." Kearney locked the monitor onto that band.

It was an odd transmission. And whoever was answering it—he could tell from the next transmission—was using a different band.

"No, Forager. The last guest was escorted. He is the Windy City man on our list. Do you copy that? Over."

Keeping only one eye on the two-lane road he

traveled, Kearney manually scanned, getting no signal, punching back to the original frequency, catching it in midtransmission. "—about—God, I don't know. Older guy, maybe in his fifties. It's the Windy City man, all right. I thought he was older. Can you confirm, Constellation? Over."

Again Kearney tried scanning, again getting nothing, but cutting back just as the transmission on the band he already had was beginning again. "Only the subject and the Windy City man, Constellation. If it is Windy City man, we save ourselves a trip and he shouldn't alter the percentages. Over."

Kearney tried again, but still got nothing. He was already activating the directional finding equipment linked to the scanner as he tuned in to the original frequency. "We will proceed on schedule starting at oh six hundred, Constellation. Have pickup for us and some hot coffee. Gonna be cold tonight." A little laughter. "Forager out."

Kearney pulled over onto the rather minimal gravel shoulder. At the back of his mind, he could hear the controller who'd dispatched him there saying "Look, old man—some suspicious radio traffic and all that. You have a job to do. Do it."

Would this be doing it?

The bearing on the transmission was southeast. To reach a highway going in that direction—he consulted his maps—he would have to double back ten miles or go on another twenty-five. He glanced into the sideview mirror and elected the second option.

That way his conscience would be clear because he'd be going in the proper direction anyway.

Kearney stomped the gas pedal.

Luther Steel's wife cried as he held her. "When I heard, Luther—my God, I thought maybe—"

The voice beside him, Rocky Saddler's voice, cut in. "They haven't made the missile that's got his name on it."

"Who—" Deana began.

"This is Rocky Saddler, a good friend and—"

"Daddy!" The voices were like a chorus and Luther Steel, still holding his wife around the waist, spun toward the sound. His children ran down from the porch of the small house. One of the Marshals Service men dodged to let them pass, smiling as he did so.

"Daddy!"

Luther Steel dropped to his knees and hugged them close.

CHAPTER TWELVE

Thomas Ashbrooke told the driver *"Danke"* as he handed over the fare and a modest tip as he stepped from the back of the taxi. He was usually a lavish tipper, but to have spent extravagantly would have left a clearer impression in the driver's mind, and the less the driver remembered him, the better. Just another foreign tourist in Berlin. There were many.

His bag in his left hand, Ashbrooke dug his right hand into his pocket. Two yellow lights illuminated the old apartment building before him. If he'd taken the time, there was a place he could have gotten a gun. He didn't take the time and now, standing all alone on the rain-slicked street in the howling wind, he almost wished that he had.

The taxicab pulled away.

The wind was stiff and it was cold. The winter

would be as cold as the summer had been hot. He turned up the collar of his leather jacket, trying to remember how many hours ago—days—it had been since he'd taken a shower or slept in a bed.

He shrugged off the thought as he walked across the sidewalk toward the doorway. It wasn't quite cold enough for the rainwater to be freezing into ice. By dawn the sidewalks and roads would be ice coated if the precipitation kept up or the wind died down. And so would the runways. He didn't know where Jurgen Staudenmeier would lead him. He doubted it would be Berlin.

His gloved hand touched at the door handle and the glass-fronted door opened. The foyer was unlighted, so Ashbrooke took a small flashlight from his shirt pocket and twisted it on. The foyer seemed clean, and nothing seemed to be scurrying out of the light across the red and white linoleum-tiled floor.

Ashbrooke swept the light over the names beside the door buzzers. The name he searched for was Fritz Klein. Finding it, he pressed the buzzer beside it and waited.

After a few seconds, Ashbrooke pressed the buzzer again.

The inner door of the foyer buzzed and opened. Ashbrooke, still holding his flight bag, walked toward the doorway, passed through, and closed the door after himself.

A stairway about wide enough for two average-size people to walk abreast angled upward.

Ashbrooke started up and stopped as he turned

the first landing. Jurgen Staudenmeier stood just above him, right hand behind his back, wearing nothing but an athletic shirt and a pair of faded blue jeans. "Ahh—my old friend Fritz Klein!" Ashbrooke smiled.

Staudenmeier moved his right hand forward. Just as Ashbrooke had anticipated he held a gun, but the pistol was not held at all menacingly. "Come up, please." Staudenmeier smiled back.

Ashbrooke took the next flight of stairs, Staudenmeier disappearing from its head just as Ashbrooke reached the top. Ashbrooke followed with his eyes for a moment as Staudenmeier—barefoot—walked down the hallway toward the open doorway at the corridor's end. The gun, now stuffed in the small of Staudenmeier's back, was a Walther P-5, Ashbrooke noticed without consciously trying to.

Ashbrooke walked along the center of the hallway, a nearly threadbare runner under his feet. He stopped at the open doorway. Staudenmeier sat at a small table just inside. On the left side of the table was a bottle of American whiskey, on the right side the pistol. "Come in," Staudenmeier said.

Ashbrooke stepped inside and closed the door, tossing his flight bag onto a straightback wooden chair just beside the door.

There was a chair identical to it facing Staudenmeier at the table and Ashbrooke walked over to it. "You always did like Walthers, Jurgen,"

Ashbrooke told him, eyeing the pistol for a moment. "How are you doing?"

"Ah, well enough. Smuggling isn't what it used to be, Thomas."

"Nothing's what it used to be. I understand your merchandise has changed over the years."

Staudenmeier shrugged his shoulders and laughed a little hollowly. "One must change with the times, my friend. Years ago guns, then later on cigarettes and American liquor. Now it's the white powder. Who knows what it will be tomorrow?"

"I'd always thought the drug business paid better," Ashbrooke remarked, gesturing around the sparsely furnished apartment.

"It usually does. I lost a shipment. Damnedest thing, Thomas. Now not only are the fucking police after me, but so are the people I was shipping it for."

"If you need money, Jurgen, I can help you out. I need information, a contact. Maybe you can help me out," Ashbrooke suggested.

"How did you find me?"

"I checked with an old friend who's one of those 'fucking police' you referred to." Staudenmeier stood up so rapidly the chair he was sitting on tumbled backward. As his hand went to close on the 9mm pistol on the table beside him, Ashbrooke's hand closed over his. "Leave it, Jurgen. He's an old friend, but not as old a friend as you. But he's nearly as corrupt. They are planning to hit your place in—" He consulted the Rolex on his wrist. "Oh, about an hour and forty minutes from now. That gives us a few minutes to chat, a few minutes for me to provide you with some traveling money and some expense money and who knows what other amounts of money for worthwhile purposes. All you have to do is give me some information. Otherwise, you can run but you don't have the money to go anywhere. I checked that."

"If you have all that money—well, why couldn't I just take some from you, Thomas, as a loan of course?"

Ashbrooke smiled. He walked over toward the window behind the table, eyeing Jurgen Staudenmeier's reflection in its blackness. The car had already pulled up across the street. "Well, I might try to stop you. Although I have been out of things for a while and you might get past me. But you wouldn't get past my corrupt policeman friend outside. Come and take a look."

Ashbrooke watched Staudenmeier approach in the window's reflection. "You shit—"

"No. So long as I leave with you before an hour and forty-five minutes elapse, he won't do a thing, Jurgen. But if you leave ahead of me, well, you're in deep shit. You can't leave after me either. He thought of that. It was a little unflattering, but he suggested that you might overpower me, take my clothes, and try to get out passing as me. Imagine that, will you?" He looked into Jurgen Staudenmeier's face, but the smuggler wasn't amused.

"What do you want to know, Thomas? Whatever it is, I need a lot of money."

Ashbrooke walked back to the table and sat down. A hard chair was a welcome relief after the airline seats and the springless taxi ride. Staudenmeier righted his fallen chair and sat down as well. "Drink?" He gestured toward the bottle of whiskey.

"No—but thanks. I don't know where what you'll tell me will take me and I don't know what condition I'll have to be in. Besides, I had a couple of drinks on the flight over."

"Switzerland?"

"America."

"How's your daughter—she lives there, doesn't she?"

Ashbrooke felt something akin to a stab wound and closed his eyes for an instant. Of course, Jurgen didn't know. "She was killed some time back, Jurgen. So were my grandchildren."

"Diane must have—*mein Gott.*"

"Yes. We all took it very hard. Our son-in-law took it harder than anyone. He's the reason I'm here."

"She was killed and you want to get the bastards?" Staudenmeier suggested, lighting a cigarette.

"I hadn't thought of doing that—at least not more than a dozen times a day, but Diane—well, if something had happened to me after the loss of Elizabeth and the grandchildren . . . I didn't. Maybe I should have. Apparently I won't have much choice. I mean, I'll never get the actual people who did it. They might be dead already. But the ones responsible—what I'm doing now might get me to them. So you'd be helping in that way too, Jurgen. She was killed by the Front for the Liberation of North America. And I want you to tell me some things."

Jurgen Staudenmeier licked his lips, took a drink. "Are you certain—about the drink?"

"I'm sure—about everything."

"I—"

"Don't tell me you don't know—"

"Yes, but, well—" Staudenmeier fell silent.

"I will tell you what has happened, Jurgen. My son-in-law is one of the leaders of the Patriots, the group fighting against the FLNA. You've heard of them, of course." Staudenmeier only nodded. Ashbrooke continued. "He came into conflict with a certain fellow who uses the alias 'Mr. Johnson'—but his real name may be Dimitri Borsoi. He's a—" Before Ashbrooke could get the word "professional" out of his mouth, Jurgen Staudenmeier's jaw seemed literally to drop, his demeanor entirely changed. "What do you know about him?"

"Leave him alone; that's what I know. You came to pay for advice. I will give you that advice for free because you are my friend. He would kill you without batting an eye. He was the best they had—"

"The KGB?" Ashbrooke said softly.

Staudenmeier poured himself another drink. His hand shook a little, but Ashbrooke charted it off to exhaustion at the late hour on Staudenmeier's part. "He was. He was expelled by the KGB. And then they tried to kill him."

"Expelled by the KGB. For what? I mean, they aren't exactly an honor society."

Jurgen Staudenmeier laughed. "Oh, he had high marks, Borsoi did. Very high. He worked with their terrorist network. He was the best."

"Then—"

"Why did they expel him and why didn't they kill him?" Staudenmeier downed half his fresh drink. "I will tell you why, Thomas. They expelled him while he was overseas. They attempted to kill him then. Because they were afraid of him. They were afraid that he would either come back and try to get them, or that he would use his people against Soviet interests. The Americans and the Russians—they are all so fond of each other these days, are they not? But Borsoi did not want this." And Staudenmeier stabbed his finger against the tabletop.

"So the KGB," Ashbrooke theorized aloud, "wanted him removed as a potential embarrassment, then?"

"No—more than that. The Russians have always feared what would happen if the Moslem minorities in their rather heterogenous country were to organize and rebel. Borsoi was the man who could have sparked this rebellion. He might still. But there were elements within the Soviet Union that wished the downfall of their own government. Not because they wanted a nuclear war. And they did not care what happened with the Moslems either. They were like you and me, Thomas. They loved money. And an easing of world tensions, even the possible cooperation of the United States and the Soviet Union, would cut off their sources of revenue."

Thomas Ashbrooke just looked at Staudenmeier. "You'll have to spell it out for me. Maybe I'm a little slow today. I'm tired. What—"

"The arms, the drugs that are used to purchase the arms, all of it—who controls it? These men. If there were to be an end to hostilities between the United States and the Soviet Union, if the Cold War were to dissolve like so much—" He lighted a cigarette. "Like so much smoke, Thomas—these men would have been back to government salaries, might even have been discovered. The West has no—what is the word?"

"Monopoly?" Ashbrooke suggested emotionlessly.

"Like the game, yes—the West has no monopoly on men who want money and power. Because all that time, Borsoi not only worked for the KGB but for them. For them, Thomas. Where would a policeman be without crime? Where would a soldier be without the threat of war? Using Borsoi and men like him—although no one is quite like him—these men he worked for could keep tensions high, keep their pockets filled."

Ashbrooke fell silent for a moment, then said, "Borsoi is using drugs, I understand, to finance the

FLNA. Or Borsoi's superiors are. How certain can you be that Borsoi is the top man?"

"Not certain at all. He is a killer, not a thinker. He probably isn't the top man, but he probably could kill the top man and perhaps replace him. He is very deadly. I met him once. The KGB was trading opium out of the Golden Triangle for a weapons system they wanted. You would never deal in narcotics, would you, Thomas?"

"They're dirty, Jurgen."

"But smuggling the other things—that is clean?"

"I never said that," Ashbrooke told him honestly. "What was he like, Borsoi?"

"Very businesslike, very polite, almost charming. But there was something about him. You've met men like him. Gestapo types, the veneer of civilization and courtesy with the flesh-hungry animal beneath." Staudenmeier paused, exhaled, studied his drink and set it down. He stubbed out his cigarette and wiped the palms of his hands across his face, as though he were washing himself. He looked up, his eyebrows rising as he smiled. "Look, Thomas. You say he is using drugs to finance what he does. Then the man who can put you on his trail—"

"My son-in-law was kidnapped by him. But there's very good reason to believe he wouldn't have killed David because he wants what's in his head or maybe wants to turn him. If he was going to keep David alive, control him—"

"The only man who might tell you anything,

Thomas, is Theron Hyde. In London. He is the man who brokers it all."

Theron Hyde. Ashbrooke knew the name. "He's a smuggler too."

"Not anymore. You have been out of the business too long, Thomas. Theron Hyde is the broker who arranges the really big deals between the elements of the global terrorist network and the drug trade. If it is happening and he doesn't know about it or have some interest in it, it isn't big. If you wish to know more about this son-in-law of yours and what has happened to him, or about Borsoi and his organization, then you must see Theron Hyde. And he will not be easy to see, even for you. He is filthy rich, this man. And he is very conscious of his security, I think."

Staudenmeier lighted another cigarette. Ashbrooke started to speak. Staudenmeier cut him off. "We are friends, you and I. But I need money to travel on and to start over again. Do you have five thousand? Dollars?"

"Yes. Traveler's checks will have to do."

"I can get them cashed. But it is a loan you are making me, Thomas. I do not charge a friend for helping him. You and Diane are still at the same house?"

"Yes."

"Then, one day soon, a package will arrive there for you. I hope you find what you are looking for, Thomas."

"So do I," Ashbrooke told him. "Now." And

Thomas Ashbrooke stood up. "I believe you and I have to leave this building. We can share a ‹ ‹ᵇ part of the way unless you have a car."

"A cab," Staudenmeier declared.

"You wouldn't be going out to the airport, would you? I'm flying to London myself as soon as I can arrange it."

Staudenmeier started to smile and Ashbrooke lighted a cigarette.

Theron Hyde.

CHAPTER THIRTEEN

Moe and Bob were ready with the machine gun, and Harry and his men had already crossed the bridge on foot. Rose Shepherd looked at the Timex Ironman watch on her left wrist. Their explosives placement should be almost complete.

It was deep twilight now, the sun gone but a purple wash of light still lingering on the western horizon.

In the bridge control house there had been some girlie magazines and a single copy of *Petersen's Handguns.* She hadn't read a gun magazine in months (she was half surprised there wasn't some sort of law against publishing them these days and was confident there would be as soon as self-appointed President Roman Makowski got around to it). She refused to dirty her hands on the girlie magazines and, to keep from chain smoking and generally going insane, she read through the gun magazine instead. There were several articles by her favorite gun writer. Jan Libourel's erudite and engaging style, sparked with subtle witticisms, had always attracted her. She had hoped to meet him someday; but, all things considered, she doubted she ever would. Like all good writing, it momentarily lifted her thoughts from her own troubles and, when she finished the article, she experienced a momentary sadness at returning to reality.

The reality was that Harry and his demolitions squad were running late.

Moe and Bob were taking turns watching the road leading from the warehouse. At any moment, the FLNA personnel, who kept relatively regular hours to avert suspicion, would be starting out for the bridge.

Rose Shepherd put down the gun magazine and fingered the walkie-talkie. "Hell with it!" she hissed under her breath. "Trapeze calling Tumbler. Trapeze calling Tumbler. Come in, Tumbler."

There was nothing but static for a moment and she started to adjust the squelch, but then Harry's voice came back. "Trapeze, this is Tumbler. All set here in about sixty seconds. Ready for you to do your thing. Over."

"This is Trapeze. Roger and out." She put down the radio. Bob was looking up from the machine gun that was set in the main window of the bridge house, commanding this side of the span from the street to the center of the bridge. "Harry's all set," Rose told him.

Moe was watching the street through the binoculars. "And not a moment too soon, Rosie. They're starting to let out."

She crossed the bridge house floor and stood beside him. Moe handed her the binoculars. After adjusting the focus slightly, she could see their faces clearly. They looked like ordinary working men, except for the longer than average hair some of them had and the younger than average unshaven faces of some others. And there were some women as well.

When the garage had first been discovered, several means were used to confirm that the personnel working there—repairing, maintaining, repainting —weren't just employees but were actual FLNA personnel. When it was confirmed independently through several sources, the initial stages of planning to hit the garage began. If it hadn't been possible to confirm that the personnel working at the warehouse garage were FLNA, any attempts to destroy the facility would have been designed to do so after the building was cleared. But this way, both the building and vehicles it housed along with as many as several dozen FLNA personnel could be eliminated at once.

And there were, by rough count, some thirty FLNA personnel in the warehouse parking lot. Singly, or by twos and threes, they entered cars and vans. A little bottleneck of traffic formed at the guarded parking lot entrance for a moment. Next they would be heading onto the bridge. "Bob—be ready. They're coming."

Rose Shepherd handed back the binoculars, Moe joining Bob on the machine gun. She picked up the radio handset, waiting for Harry to come in. Where was he? Had something gone wrong in the few seconds— "Trapeze, this is Tumbler. Do you copy my transmission? Over."

"Tumbler, this is Trapeze. I copy. Go ahead. Over."

"Count to ten. I say again—count to ten. Now. Out."

She pouched the radio to her belt, grabbing up her M-16 from the table.

"Nine seconds until the explosives go. Then we've got 'em."

Cars were already starting out onto the bridge. About half of the FLNA personnel were in the prime killing zone; the remainder were entering it. She went to the bridge controls, waiting.

Seven seconds remained.

Six.

"Most of 'em are on the bridge, Rosie," Bob sang out.

"Not yet." Five seconds. Now four.

Moe shouted, "I see another vehicle coming up near the warehouse along the side. Could be Harry."

"Could be—take cover, then get your eyes back on the target, Moe."

One second. "Protect yourselves!" She dropped to

her knees on the floor behind the desk and pulled her poncho over her. The sound of the explosion was ear-splittingly loud, but the sound of the glass in the bridge house windows blowing inward seemed louder. She felt the glass as it pelted against the poncho and for an instant questioned her decision not to bring heavier coverings to protect them. She also questioned herself for not taking shelter under the desk. But there wasn't room under there for the two men with her, and to have protected herself more— She felt the silence, then moved, glass sliding from her as she doffed the poncho.

"Hit it!" Rose Shepherd shouted.

Bob was on the M-60, and he opened up with Moe beside him to help service the gun. Burning-hot brass flew everywhere, pelting at her as she ran to the bridge controls and activated them. She moved behind Bob and Moe to the other window overlooking the bridge. With the butt of her M-16, she hammered out two dagger-size shards of glass that hadn't been knocked out by the force of the explosion. And, for the first time, she looked toward the warehouse.

A gigantic fireball was still rising above the building, the warehouse itself consumed with flames, the flames licking upward, drawn into the heat rush. Burning debris littered the warehouse parking lot. She could see no sign of Harry and his two men from the demolitions team.

There was no time to worry about them more than she had already. Rose Shepherd stabbed the

M-16 through the blown-in window and opened fire. The alarm bell was sounding, signaling the bridge was rising. A red and white striped barricade arm, like those used at railroad crossings, was lowered. Some of the FLNA vehicles at the entrance to the bridge were trying to back up or turn around. The arm came down over the windshield of a van, shattering the windshield glass as the arm bounced upward, then downward to strike it again.

The first thirty-round magazine in the M-16 was spent. Windows of many vehicles were shot out, and a few of the FLNAers who had abandoned their vehicles were down, either to her gunfire or that of the M-60.

She heard the radio on her belt, swapping magazines as she tucked down, racking the M-16's action, then taking the radio. "This is Trapeze, Tumbler. What's your ten-twenty? Over."

"Two hundred yards back from the warehouse. We lost our windshield and had to liberate a second vehicle. No one was hurt. What's your situation? Over."

"The plan is working. Hang back and wait for my signal. Trapeze out."

She pouched the radio again, then was up to her knees, firing the M-16. "Keep it up, Rosie!" It was Bob shouting. "Gotta clear a jam!" She burned out the M-16's magazine, buttoned it out, rammed a fresh one home. She began firing again. There was answering fire from the base of the bridge. Chunks of window molding ripped away, little fragments of glass left from the implosion showering around her. She closed her eyes against it, tucking down.

More gunfire. Rose Shepherd stabbed the M-16 over the window frame, not looking, just spraying right and left and downward.

"We got her fixed!" Moe shouted. The M-60 machine gun began firing again. Rosie drew her hand back, plucked a piece of glass off her sleeve, and loaded another magazine up the well of the M-16.

Almost time for the gas grenades. Almost.

She peered up over the window frame. The bridge was nearly fully upright. Some of the cars and vans that had already ventured onto it before Bob and Moe had opened fire were beginning to roll backward, tires squealing, leaving smoldering black drags behind them. A van, trying to turn around, overturned and rolled down, smashing into other fleeing vehicles. As the van hit the bottom of the bridge, Rose screamed, "Look out!" to Bob and Moe. The explosion shook the bridge house walls, and Rose averted her eyes as more glass spewed inward. As she looked out again, the van and two cars were at the base of a fire and gasoline was tracking from still another vehicle.

She grabbed the radio from her belt. "Tumbler. This is Trapeze. Come now. Acknowledge. Over."

"Trapeze. This is Tumbler. Wilco that. On the way. Out."

The stream of gasoline was nearly to the burning van and the two cars. Rose Shepherd was up, pouching the radio as she ran to the bridge controls. "Moe! Bob! Get ready to move that gun, fast!"

She was at the bridge controls. As she activated them the alarm sounded again. She ran toward the bag of gas grenades stashed out of the way of stray gunfire behind an upended metal table. She reached over, grabbing the sack.

The alarm that the bridge was lowering was sounding again.

When she reached the window, Moe had the Hawk MM 1 grenade launcher ready. It was the length of a stubby sawed-off shotgun or a sub-machine gun, a cylinder about the size of a tricycle wheel circling it. She crouched beside Moe as he shifted the MM 1 into the open window, fired, fired again and again and again. The cylinder rotated each time until at last it was empty.

The gas was already forming a cloud that covered the base of the bridge road. She started handing Moe more of the gas grenades from the sack. As he reloaded, she stabbed the M-16 she held in her other hand through the window, firing into the gas cloud.

"Loaded," Moe snapped.

"Bob—mask up. We're moving!"

She rammed a fresh magazine up the well of the M-16, then grabbed the gas mask from the bag at her side, pulled it on over her face, inhaling, exhaling, and snapping the cheeks to seal it. Then she moved to the door.

She went through first, firing a short burst into the street.

Moe was next, firing the Hawk MM 1—it was potentially one of the most useful things they'd ever taken from the FLNA.

The gas filled the entire street and obscured the bridge itself.

There was an explosion—it had to be the van and the two burning cars; the stream of gasoline must have finally hit them. A wall of flame was suddenly there, blocking the base of the bridge. Cars were already crossing through it, some of them on fire, speeding onto the bridge. One car—a battered gray four-door sedan that was already on fire—spun out as it neared the center of the bridge, hit the guard rail, and bounced over the side, plunging into the river below.

Rose Shepherd ran down the steps toward the bridge level, the tear gas billowing around her.

The radio on her belt was talking to her. "Trapeze —I see you. It's the blue Dodge van with the trashed right fender."

She spun toward the street. She could see the blue van, waved toward Harry.

Moe was emptying the MM 1 again. At the base of the steps, the M-60 machine gun cradled in his arms, Bob was firing toward the gas cloud. The fire that had blocked the base of the bridge was nearly dissipated now.

The blue van slowed, stopped, the side door already open. She could see Harry behind the wheel, bringing a gas mask to his face.

Rose Shepherd ran for the van. She dropped to

one knee beside it and covered Bob and Moe with her M-16 as they ran for the van.

They were inside.

She jumped in after them, her rifle empty. "Hit it, Harry!"

But the van was already moving.

She put aside the empty assault rifle, drawing David's Desert Eagle from the Southwind Sanctions holster on her thigh. She thumbed back the hammer.

As the van passed onto the bridge, an FLNAer jumped toward the open side door. "Mine!" Rose shouted to the men in the van. She fired, the Desert Eagle's muzzle snapping upward. The recoil was not that severe but the noise was deafening in the confined space of the van, and her ears rang more than they already had.

The FLNAer fell away.

Bob set up the M-60 in the open doorway, Rose Shepherd crouched beside him.

They passed an FLNA van, stalled at the center of the bridge.

Bob opened fire. Rose aimed the Desert Eagle at the van's windshield and fired, then again and again, shattering the windshield. Bob's machine-gun fire strafed across the van's right side.

"We're nearly there!" Harry shouted, his voice sounding oddly muffled from under the gas mask.

She looked forward; the end of the bridge was in sight.

Any moment police or military helicopters would

be over the bridge. She didn't want to wait for them. Rose Shepherd took the radio from her belt pouch. "This is Trapeze calling Adaggio, over."

"This is Adaggio, Trapeze. Reading you loud and clear. Traffic proceeding as expected through the funnel, over."

"I copy that, Adaggio. Trapeze out."

Patsy Alfredi was in position, routing all the FLNA vehicles that had gotten over the bridge in the opposite direction from the one Harry would drive.

They were off the bridge, Harry making a tight right, Bob nearly losing the M-60 through the open doorway.

"Shut the door!" Rose Shepherd ordered.

She realized the Desert Eagle was still in her right hand, still cocked. But she'd safed it.

She sat back, worked the magazine release, drew back the slide to clear the chamber, and lowered the hammer. She loaded the ejected round into the top of the magazine.

She'd done it.

Nobody on the Patriot side killed or injured, the warehouse blown, the loss in FLNA vehicles and lives substantial.

And there was no pursuit—at least not yet.

Rose Shepherd stripped off the gas mask, coughed, feeling a little light-headed.

"Shit, Rosie! You did it!" Harry shouted, laughing.

Bob clapped her on the shoulder. Moe punched her gently in the left arm. "All right, boss!"

She took a cigarette from the pocket of her BDUs and lighted it, inhaling deeply. She didn't want to be the boss. She wanted David back. She could have cried.

CHAPTER FOURTEEN

Geoffrey Kearney pulled to the side of the road, reactivating the scanning monitor. He was safely out of sight of the police roadblock he'd passed through two miles back where he and his car were searched. He had the monitor locked into the same frequency as before. Nothing.

But the transmission had clearly sounded ominous, the reference to "Windy City man" too enigmatic to be casual, and the quality of the transmission indicated expensive equipment. Circumstantial evidence, at best.

But its origin had been in the same direction he'd intended traveling—more or less, at least. He left the scanning monitor on now, checking the sideview mirror, then turned off the shoulder and back onto the highway, cursing his own idiocy and meddling.

* * *

The man from the Marshals Service—the deputy who had been on the front porch when Steel first arrived—sat on the sofa, reading an update bulletin. The other deputy, a woman, very pretty in a Scandinavian sort of way, was out patrolling the grounds.

Rocky Saddler was out patrolling the grounds with her. Saddler was no fool.

Steel's wife, Deana, entered the room, carrying a small tray with a glass of whiskey and a cup of coffee on it. She bent over beside Steel—he sat in the easy chair beside the still fireplace—and he took the glass of whiskey. He rarely drank, but felt he could use a drink tonight. If Rocky was right, however, and there was to be an attempt . . . He sipped at the whiskey, saying "Thanks, honey." It would be the only drink he'd allow himself.

She brought the marshal, a man in his late twenties, not very tall, dark-haired and eyed, the cup of coffee. "Thanks, Mrs. Steel."

"Join us, Deana?" Steel called out as his wife started back toward the kitchen.

"Couple of minutes, Luther—kids need me." And she was gone.

"You've got a lovely wife, Agent Steel," the marshal volunteered.

"Thank you, Deputy. You married?"

"Marriage and the Marshals Service go pretty poorly together. But I'll probably try it sometime."

Steel smiled, saying "Not the easiest thing in the world being married and working for the Bureau either." Steel was eager to talk, about anything. "That a Smith & Wesson 645 you're carrying?"

"A 4506, they call it. Third-generation Smith. Ever try one?"

"No—my SIG-Sauer and I get along great."

The marshal smiled. "I like a bigger bullet, that's all. SIG's a good gun."

"What's the lady deputy carry?"

"Olga?"

"Yeah—Olga." Steel congratulated himself on the Scandinavian deduction.

"If she's restricted to purse carry, she has one of those little snubby Smith & Wessons like you have in that shoulder holster."

"A sixty-six?"

"Yeah, that's it. But for stuff like this, she carries a four-inch L-Frame, stainless one. She's a revolver man—person—all the way."

"Been pretty quiet around here?" Steel asked.

"We've never lost a witness protection subject yet. We treat your family the same way, Agent Steel."

"Luther—use my first name."

"Jim."

"Jim—look, ah—"

"The best way you can help, Luther, is just to relax and let us do our job. You can bank on it if something goes down, we'll get you helping. But nothing should go down. So, just relax and enjoy your family."

Steel smiled, sipped at his drink. The revolver was unloaded and on the mantel, his ammo in his pants pocket. The automatic was in his waistband holster. Relax, he thought.

The transmission came again. He recognized the voice and this time, the signal was stronger. He was closer. No pro words this time, more like a chat instead. "I see the blonde. You see her?"

"Yeah. The old black guy's with her. What the hell's that gun he's got?"

"Looks like some kinda sub. Shut up about that stuff in case anybody's listening. You about ready?"

"Just about."

"Call me."

The transmission went dead. And this time, both ends had been on the same band.

The first time, Kearney theorized, his eyes on the road, his mind on the transmission, the speaker had been dealing with a superior. But the speaker was part of a group. And within the group, everyone was on the same frequency. Maybe, Kearney thought, he was quite close.

The direction was the same. He kept driving.

The children were in bed. The male deputy, Jim, had left the house; the female deputy, Olga, took his place. They would be changing watches in an hour. Rocky Saddler was in the kitchen, making himself an omelet. Deana had volunteered to make it for him, but he'd just told her to relax.

"He's an odd old man," Deana said, looking up from her needlepoint. "But I like him."

Steel put the videotape on pause—it was one of his favorite John Wayne westerns—and looked at his wife more intently. "He's a neat old guy. And tough too. Good friend of Mr. Cerillia's. He's a Congressional Medal of Honor winner."

"Ohh—I always thought that the only men who got those," she said, "were dead."

Steel smiled. "Most of them are—I mean, in most cases, as far as I've always understood, the men who win them die winning them. He's an exceptional man."

"I couldn't help overhearing you," the woman deputy said, tossing her hair back off her shoulders as she looked up from her magazine. "Then he's the one?"

"The one?"

"The Rocky Saddler I read about. I thought he'd be a lot older."

Steel smiled. "He's older than he looks." He hoped the casual remark that just escaped his lips wouldn't queer things for Saddler with her.

"He was quite the hero. I'm tempted to ask for his autograph." Olga smiled.

"Oh, me too," Deana enthused.

Steel just shook his head and took the VCR off pause. The Duke was in a tough spot, but Steel—who'd seen the movie several dozen times over the years—was confident of the outcome.

The scanning monitor was capable of judging signal amplitude and, therefore, direction and, at close range, distance. The distance and direction finders weren't that precise, but precise enough. As Kearney stepped out of the car and looked down the road, he realized whoever was making the transmissions had to be somewhere in the woods surrounding the farmhouse that was just visible by its lights.

Another FLNA attack?

They didn't sound like disenchanted punks. The voices on the radio sounded mature, confident. Who was the "Windy City man" and why was he carrying a submachine gun?

Geoffrey Kearney took his gloves from his pocket. Time to get one or two little things from the car, then time to find out.

CHAPTER FIFTEEN

The night sky was crystal clear and Luther Steel—
he was sure much to the consternation of the new
team of deputies who'd come on duty—stood with
Deana on the front porch, watching the stars.

The new deputies seemed, by contrast to Jim and
Olga, rather blah, he thought. Both men, both in
their forties, both of them pleasant enough but very
quiet. Maybe that was why they worked the grave-
yard shift.

Rocky Saddler lay across the couch, asleep. The
deputies had balked at the man being armed. Steel
had told them that he'd vouch for Saddler's charac-
ter.

Deana said, "I'm cold."

"Cold, huh? I bet."

"You think I just want you to put your arms around me, don't you?"

"I was kind of hoping." Steel smiled.

"Me too." She smiled. He drew his wife close to him, touched his lips to her forehead. "Aww, Lute."

She almost never called him that. So he called her "Dee—you been doing all right?"

"The children miss their daddy. I miss their daddy. When's this going to be over?"

He wished he could tell her. "It's going to be over for me pretty soon, I think. Would you mind it if I weren't in the FBI any more? I mean, could you live with me being home most of the time, making two or three times as much money? Like that?"

She leaned her head against his chest. He smiled. It was the most pleasant realization in the world that he could still get a hard on just by holding her close, just like when they were kids, even after being married to her all these years. "You don't want to quit the Bureau," she whispered. "Why are they doing this to Mr. Cerillia? He seemed so nice that time I met him."

"He's a good man. Maybe that's why the new President—I shouldn't talk that way. He's the President."

"But he's not a good man, is he, Luther?"

"I don't think so."

"What about your friends in the Task Force? What will they do, Luther?"

Luther Steel looked into her eyes. They were prettier than the stars. "All of them were dispatched to desk jobs. I don't know what they'll do. Clark Pietrowski's old enough to draw full pension and still good enough to get into private security work. Bill Runningdeer—I don't know. Same with Tom LeFleur. Both of them are close to my age. Not much choice but to quit, go into the private security field." There was always the possibility that President Makowksi would put something into their records—have it put there—that showed them as security risks, meaning none of them would find jobs easily. "The guy I feel the worst about is Randy Blumenthal. He's a kid. Just starting out. But maybe when one of us gets something, well—"

"You're a good man, Luther Steel. The best man I've ever met. I used to think my father was the biggest and roughest and toughest and sweetest. But then I met you. You're kind. That's important in a man. Kindness is. Do you think we'd scandalize the deputies if—"

"They look like they could use a little excitement," Steel told his wife, bringing her closer against him, kissing her hard on the mouth.

He wasn't overly warm with the SWAT black American GI M-65 field jacket. He'd left the button-in liner in the car trunk. His face was the only thing not covered in black as he moved through the woods.

Geoffrey Kearney had checked the scanning monitor once more. Whatever was about to happen, it was going to happen quickly. From the transmission, it was impossible to tell how many men were involved, but at the minimum six. He thought there were probably more, perhaps twice as many.

After better than half an hour of moving about in the woods like some sort of fool, he reassessed and determined that since the house was the obvious target—it was the only thing for several miles as far as he could tell—he would be better off watching the house.

Through the armored Zeiss binoculars, he had observed a man and woman, both of them possibly black—it was hard to tell with the shadow—standing together rather romantically on the farmhouse front porch.

For some odd reason, he thought of Harriet, cold and dead. He wanted a cigarette very badly, but couldn't now. He had put down the binoculars, feeling like a peeping Tom. Eventually the man and woman had withdrawn from the porch to the house. The romantic in him wished they'd have a pleasant liaison. But the practical side of him hoped that, if the man had a gun, he'd keep it near him. The man and woman, whoever they were, seemed the obvious target.

There had been something oddly familiar about the man, but from the distance it was impossible to tell just what. The set of the shoulders, the carriage —and it haunted him now. The man was someone he had met, and recently. But he couldn't put a face to the someone.

Why were the FLNA—logically it had to be them

albeit circumstances hinted otherwise—interested in this farmhouse? Who was the "Windy City man?"

Geoffrey Kearney settled into his tree limb notch, anticipating a long, cold night. And the fact that he had not slept for better than thirty hours was starting to tell on him.

If he allowed himself to sleep, not only was he risking his ability to intervene in the developing situation, but he was risking his very life.

One didn't fall asleep on enemy turf.

He put his rifle securely into the notch with the chamber empty and the sling entwined about his wrist. He forced himself to keep his mind on something—anything really—in order to stay awake. There was that lovely girl he'd met at Mildred Sommersett's country house. Mildred was a snob, of course, but there had been absolutely nothing else to do and even the job was simply an unending stream of paperwork. Lovely girl. He was glad he'd gone to the party. But the lovely girl had proven to be married and had told him that only after they'd spent the night together at his place. "Oh, I don't love my husband. You should know that." He had been pleased she didn't love the fellow. And probably the chap—whoever he was—was the better for it if his wife fell into bed with a man the same night she'd met him at a party.

The man and the woman he'd observed on the front porch—there seemed to be something much more permanent about them. He envied that. His sort of job—that was always the excuse he made, at least. But it wasn't the job really. He just became disappointed very easily.

He dismissed thoughts of the girl from the Sommersett party, trying to think of something else. His comparatively new pistol. He had wanted the steel-framed, stainless-steel version, the 5906, but none had been available in time for him to take with him. A stainless-steel frame lasted longer, of course, than an alloy frame. But in his line of work, such was a moot point. Still—

He'd been after the Service armorer to get him one of the smaller ones, the model number escaping him. They seemed eminently concealable, and he liked the Smith & Wesson automatics because they reminded him so much of the Walther automatics and he'd always liked those.

He smiled. He'd never met a man in British Secret Intelligence who carried a Walther PPK, à la their famous fictional counterpart. Several Walther PP pistols, a few chopped-down Walther P-38s, the excellent P-5, of course, even one chap who used a Walther P-88, their newest. But never once a fellow with a Walther PPK. And why, these days, would anyone carry a miserable little caliber like 7.65mm? There was only one decent load and the .380 variant was considerably better, even in its poorest configuration.

But, like virtually everyone he knew in the Service, when a new film came out, he was one of the first to see it. Rather like a plumber going to see a film that glorified plumbers, he suspected.

In the real Service there were never the girls, there was never the budget.

It was rather discouraging to leave the theater afterward. Although, if someone asked, "I say, are you a spy?" since the Official Secrets Act forbade answering in the affirmative he was saved the embarrassment that came from his car not being wildly curvacious and expensive, nor his woman. And although he owned a Rolex, if the watch was smashed or something he'd be stuck paying to replace it himself.

What he really envied was the gadgets. The scanning monitor with its in-built directional finder was the wildest gadget anyone in the Service had ever provided for his use. No flying motorcycles or expensive cars capable of taking on a Soviet armored division.

He wondered if he could have taken it. "Here—take this bomb. It's the size of a cufflink, why we shaped it like one. It will have a destructive radius of forty meters. Do try and return it, old man." None of that.

He checked with the binoculars again. Only a downstairs light was on in the farmhouse.

He glanced at the Rolex on his wrist. It was getting on toward 9 P.M. He shrugged. At least the Rolex he wore was his own.

CHAPTER SIXTEEN

Luther Steel rolled over when he opened his eyes. Why had he awakened? A strange bed in a strange house. That wasn't the reason.

He sat bolt upright so quickly that his wife began to stir beside him. "Go back to sleep, Deana," Steel whispered, his right hand leaving her thigh and crossing to the bedside table and the SIG-Sauer P-226 9mm there. There was no reason to suppose that he would need the pistol, but sometimes, when it came to staying alive, instinct had to be listened to over reason.

Because there were children in the house—his children—he'd left the pistol chamber empty. He drew the slide back slowly, then thumbed down the decocking lever as soon as the slide returned to battery. He placed the loose round he'd taken from the

SIG's chamber in the magazine and quickly rein-
serted the magazine up the butt of the pistol.

What had he heard? What had awakened him?

"Lute?"

"Go back to sleep, Dee," Steel told her.

Naked, he slipped out from beneath the covers,
grateful for his blackness, like the blackness around
him. This time he heard the noise, really heard it, in
the distance, indefinable, outside the house—maybe.
His trousers were on the chair a few feet from the
bed and he took them in hand now, eyeing the doorway. What had awakened him? That noise?

He pulled his pants on, stuffing the pistol into his
waistband. The metal was cold against his abdomen.
Steel loaded the little Smith & Wesson revolver that
he carried in the shoulder holster with the six
rounds that were still loose in his pants pocket and
placed it beside his wife on the bedside table. Just in
case.

"Deana—there's a loaded gun next to—"

"Luther?"

"I heard something. Just stay in bed. First sign of
trouble, get to the kids and keep them with you.
Nothing's getting down this hallway. Trust me. And
don't cock the revolver. Too easy to have an AD—"

"A what?"

"Accidental discharge."

"Be careful," she said needlessly. He always was.

Luther Steel went to the doorway and glanced
back at Deana sitting up with the covers drawn up
under her chin. He smiled at her, doubted she could

see the gesture, then slowly opened the door, the SIG in his right fist. Deana wouldn't have seen it. And he was glad, because the sight of a gun ready in his hand might have frightened her more than she probably was already.

The origin of the noise could have been one of the marshals moving around. Or Rocky Saddler, although Steel doubted he would have heard the old veteran. For that matter, it could have been one of the children.

He didn't think that it had been deputy marshals or Rocky Saddler or wandering children. Both his four-year-old and his six-year-old had been sound sleepers ever since birth. He only felt something that scared him. He went out into the hallway to meet it, whatever it was.

He'd fallen asleep, but whatever sixth sense it was that had kept him alive all these years awakened him now.

Geoffrey Kearney's left hand was asleep from the wrist down, the sling from the CAR-15 having been bound around his wrist too tightly.

He closed his eyes tightly and opened them.

It had to have been a sound. He'd never slept with his eyes open. So he remained perfectly still, trying to focus his eyes on the house.

He saw movement in the shadows to the right side of the house coming from the trees. The movement was so quick, so subtle, that it might have been an animal. Even though he was no authority on the fauna of the upper midwestern United States, he didn't think it was an animal.

Kearney's left hand began to flex, his right hand slowly moving the offending sling away, lifting the CAR-15, easing the weight. He started massaging his wrist above and below the band of his Rolex. The CAR-15 was across his lap, the sling looped over his right elbow so the gun wouldn't fall from the tree. He was still not fully awake and was angry with himself.

He saw the movement again, but this time on the other side of the house. It was definitely a man. And this was definitely the place the mysterious voices he'd heard over the scanning monitor referred to. The possibility had not escaped him that what he had overheard were law enforcement or security personnel simply preparing for a raid against the FLNA, or drug dealers or something like that. But his experiences with constituted law hadn't been all that pleasant since his clandestine arrival the previous night.

"Oh, for a starlight scope," Kearney murmured all but inaudibly under his breath.

CHAPTER SEVENTEEN

Rose Shepherd watched the television news. Mitch Diamond had suggested tapping into a main cable line, but David had argued that the tap could be traced to them. So they had no first-run movies, just network and a few local stations off an antenna hidden in a stand of trees. But when the overcast conditions were right, the picture wasn't half bad.

The black woman who read the news—she was very pretty, very intelligent looking and even seemed compassionate—was saying "Police are revealing no new clues in the mysterious gun battle on the old bridge linking Industry Island to Metro. FLNA. Patriots. No one knows for sure, but it all started around rush-hour tonight. Patrick Hughes has the details." She even turned toward the screen behind her as if she were interested. Rose Shepherd wondered how, if no one knew for sure, Patrick Hughes could have any details at all.

"Tonight Metro police are baffled. Who tried killing whom? That is the question. But the answer seems hard to come by." They cut to videotape, apparently shot just moments after the battle. Fires were still raging from some of the cars, the gas cloud at the island side base of the bridge still quite intense. The reporter began to narrate and Rose Shepherd stood up and walked out of the main tent, into the night, pulling the M-65 field jacket closer around her shoulders. After the raid, once she knew all were accounted for and they had not been traced to what some of the Patriots almost laughingly called "The Hideout," she'd showered. It was only a sun shower and the water was cold, but she had wanted to feel clean.

She hadn't felt warm since. A pair of jeans, track shoes, a sweatshirt, and then a hot meal—she'd helped with the dishes—and she'd felt better.

She looked up at the stars. "David . . ."

When she even thought of his name, she wanted to cry.

David Holden stared into the night through the mouth of the cave where they had taken refuge. One of the horses whinnied softly. The stars seemed so close there. It was trite even to think it, but he almost did feel that if he could reach out just a bit farther, he could have touched one. It was easy to see primitive man's preoccupation with the stars, personifying the constellations, endowing them with godlike powers. Their beauty was incredible, and the sky surrounding the twinkling diamond shapes was almost the texture of velvet.

Was Rosie thinking of him? Holden wondered. He thought she was, tried telling himself that thinking that way wasn't conceit, merely confidence in the fidelity of a loved one—the loved one.

It might take weeks, even months, to get back to Metro. He didn't want anything between them to have changed. Every person needed some island of permanence; and, since the deaths of his wife and children, she had become his.

Maria turned beside him and Holden reached out, covering her again. Her fever was totally gone and she did not seem inordinately restless. He slept beside her because it was practical to sleep beside her. He hadn't touched her in a sexual way and had no intention of doing so. Fidelity was something he rarely thought of; it was a given.

He'd known guys, some of them married, who used to brag about their conquests. He'd always thought that a man was saying "Hey—I'm an asshole!" when he bragged about infidelity. If the woman the man was married to or had a relationship with was so worthless as to be cheated on, why was the man so stupid as to have a relationship with her in the first place?

With Maria sleeping against his side, huddling close to him against the cold of the high jungle night, David Holden saw only one face among the stars. And, inside of him, he knew she saw his.

CHAPTER EIGHTEEN

Luther Steel was violating the most basic rule of home defense. When a home is invaded during the night, the basic procedure is to gather all family members in one room as quickly as possible, summoning the police and notifying them that you are waiting in the bedroom or whatever room. And then you wait, everyone in as safe a position as possible behind cover with a gun ready. If the police get there first, they know where you are and the chances of being mistaken for the intruder and getting shot are considerably minimized. If the intruder reaches the strong room first, you are in a position of cover and have at least a modest advantage. Plus, there might be some potential legal advantages in the aftermath of such a shooting. You didn't go looking for the intruder with blood in your eye. He came looking for you with blood in his.

Luther Steel supposed that it was possible to practice law, the career for which he had trained. Although in the last few months he'd felt vastly older, he was still to turn thirty. But could he change careers? Did he really want to?

Never go to the prowler, the burglar, the invader; let him or them come to you in your defensive position. He'd been violating a number of rules lately, all in the name of common sense and what was right. There was no reason to stop now.

Luther Steel crept along the hallway, the SIG-Sauer P-226 balled tight in his right fist, two twenty-round spare magazines in his pants pockets.

Rocky Saddler had spooked him. Scared him.

What if Rocky Saddler was right? What if the de facto President, Roman Makowski, wanted him dead as part of a conspiracy against FBI director Rudolph Cerillia?

The noises could be no simple prowler, burgler, or home invader but a team of killers intent on his life and the lives of everyone in the house who might be a witness. Wife, children, the marshals, all of them. Rocky Saddler too.

As he moved along the corridor, he felt hands touch him, simultaneously closing over his gunhand like a vise, wedged over the hammer of his pistol so it could not be drawn back by trigger action, and over his mouth. Before he could react, he heard the voice. "Be cool, Luther. Me. Rocky," the voice rasped in his ear.

Rocky Saddler.

Luther Steel remembered to breathe.

"We've got company. Professional. You stay with me to back me up. I've got the equipment and I don't have a wife and two kids to worry about. Be cool."

His eyes well accustomed to the darkness, Luther Steel glanced into the shadows where Rocky Saddler stood. With the black face and the customary dark clothing, Rocky Saddler was virtually invisible. The TEC-9 was in Saddler's left fist, the Browning High Power in his right. These profiles Steel saw clearly. FBI hostage rescue teams used the High Power. And the TEC-9, of all the civilian legal assault pistols, was one of the simplest and the best.

Rocky Saddler was the best. Luther Steel had realized that almost from the very first.

"All right. Don't get yourself killed. It's me they want," Steel whispered hoarsely.

"Don't be a fool. If they want you, they want me, and the motherfuckers want every one of your men." And Saddler was moving.

Geoffrey Kearney was moving, along the treeline and toward the front porch of the farmhouse. More silhouettes were barely visible in the night. Not animals. Men.

In his right hand, its stock retracted, Kearney fisted the CAR-15's pistol grip. That was a feature

he liked about the CAR-15. It was as nearly maneu-
verable as a submachine gun or a large pistol at
close quarters. The 5.56mm cartridge it fired was
vastly more effective and had more penetration. He
kept moving, dropping into a crouch near the trunk
of a gnarled pine, when the flash of movement along
the front porch alerted him.

This wasn't one of the attackers, he realized. A
man, in a white shirt and tie, a submachine gun
profiled in his hands, crouched beside the porch
swing.

Who were the targets of the radio assassins?

Kearney started moving again, but deeper within
the tree cover so the man with the submachine gun
wouldn't see him.

Luther Steel, a step and a half behind Rocky Saddler, reached the base of the stairs.

Rocky moved like a cat, along the periphery of
the living room, his eyes evidently better accustomed to the darkness as well, because Steel nearly
tripped twice over pieces of furniture in still-unfa-
miliar locations.

On the porch, through the drawn-back drapes of
one of the two living-room windows, Steel could see
one of the two Marshals Service deputies.

Had this been what he'd heard?

He hoped so.

Geoffrey Kearney reached a position parallel to
the front porch. The man with the submachine gun

had taken better cover, near the door frame of the front door, in a nearly prone position. And there seemed to be a radio in one hand.

Kearney waited. Further movement would have betrayed his presence.

There was movement off to Kearney's far right, about fifty yards from the front porch, out of practical submachine gun range unless the gun was a Heckler & Kock and/or the man behind it was a superlative marksman.

The man on the porch shouted, "Identify yourself. You are trespassing on property under the protection of the United States Marshals Service!"

Kearney started to move.

The man on the porch didn't move quickly enough as assault rifle fire hammered into the area surrounding the door. The man—a deputy marshal presumably—was thrown back, his body twisting under the sustained gunfire.

Kearney retracted the stock on the CAR-15 and brought it to his shoulder.

The door opened suddenly. There was a semiautomatic burst, then another and another as hands reached out to draw the wounded or dead man inside.

Kearney held his fire.

Shadows in the darkness surrounding the house took form and substance. Men were moving to close on the house, the silhouettes of assault rifles and submachine guns visible. He could see at least a dozen attackers.

Kearney drew back deeper into the tree cover.

A burst of submachine gun fire came from the house's first floor. A window shattered on the second floor followed by submachine gun fire spraying tongues of fire into the darkness toward the attackers. Marshals Service personnel would likely work a protection detail—which this obviously was—in pairs. That meant that the second marshal was on the upper floor of the house and someone on the lower floor, perhaps another Marshals Service man or one of the persons being protected, was firing as well.

Kearney evaluated his position quickly. There was ample opportunity for lateral movement and he could always draw back more deeply into the trees.

The CAR-15 was still at his shoulder.

Kearney opened fire on one of the attackers, a quick two-round semiautomatic burst, cutting the man down. Before there could be answering fire, Kearney moved forward, along the treeline as it paralleled the side of the house.

"Let them in the house—we can get them in a crossfire from the stairs—come on," Saddler shouted, stabbing the TEC-9 that was still in his left hand through the shot-out window beside him, pumping a half-dozen semiauto shots into the darkness.

Luther Steel hauled the wounded Marshals Service man—he was still alive—up and over his shoulder, his blood sticky against Steel's bare chest. The

SIG-Sauer P-226 in his belt, Steel had the deputy's Uzi.

"That gunfire from upstairs—" Steel started.

"The second deputy. Come on." Saddler fired a few more shots and started for the stairs, shouting up "Hey, Deputy—it's Saddler and Steel. We've got your partner. He's shot up. We're going to hold the stairs. Did you hear me!"

"How bad is he?" the voice called from above.

"Bad—but alive."

"Your wife and the kids are okay, Agent Steel."

Steel breathed. He took the stairs two at a time, despite the weight of the injured man over his shoulder. Saddler was just behind him, advancing up the stairs with his back turned, the TEC-9 and the Browning High Power in his hands.

Steel reached the head of the stairs and walked into the bedroom. His wife was no longer there. He lowered the injured deputy onto the bed. He had multiple gunshot wounds and was bleeding heavily. Deana had been a nurse. "Deana—I'm coming with the injured deputy. Get the first-aid kit out of the bathroom," Steel shouted, drawing the man up into his arms. The deputy moaned in pain. At least he was still alive.

Steel was into the hallway, keeping to a low crouch. The second deputy called out, "They're in the bathroom, Agent Steel."

Deana shouted, "Luther—we're in here!"

Steel reached the bathroom. His wife crouched

beside the tub, his revolver in her hands. The children lay inside the tub flat on their faces.

"Keep them in the tub. Safer there," Steel ordered as his wife helped him get the man down to the floor.

"My God, Luther—"

"Do what you can for him." And Steel was through the door, shouting back to the kids "Mind your mother and stay down!"

Gunfire came from the first floor of the house—assault rifles, from the sound of it. Chunks of the hallway wall were blowing out. Rocky Saddler tucked into the doorway opposite Steel and his wife's bedroom, the TEC-9 like an extension of Saddler's hand, his wrist rotating right and left, firing the 9mm assault pistol down the stairwell.

Steel dodged forward, shouting to Saddler, "I'm coming!" He half threw himself through the open doorway into the bedroom, just opposite Saddler. The Uzi in his fist stabbed through the open doorway as Steel got to his knees. He fired down the stairwell. "Magazines for this thing, Deputy!"

From the rear of the hallway where the second deputy was firing down into the yard, Steel heard the voice come back, "Throw 'em to you. Be ready!"

Steel fired a short burst into the stairwell. Saddler snapped, "I'm covering you," as he rammed a fresh magazine up the well of the assault pistol. Steel tried to remember—a thirty-six-round magazine in the TEC-9? He'd ask Saddler if he lived that long.

The first magazine sailed down the hallway. Steel caught it. A second came which he almost missed.

More gunfire blasted from the base of the stairs and the hallway ceiling started to collapse in chunks.

Steel fired out the Uzi and dumped the spent magazine, replacing it with a fresh one.

They couldn't hold out much longer. And what if the attackers set fire to the house?

Steel shivered at the thought. "Who the hell are you bastards?"

The gunfire from the base of the stairwell ceased for a moment. A voice called back, laughing, "The last people you'll ever see, Agent Steel!" and then the gunfire resumed, seemed to double. There were chunks of wood and plaster flying everywhere. Steel was stabbing the Uzi down the hall and into the stairwell, firing wildly because he couldn't see.

Saddler shouted. "They're rushing us, Luther!"

Steel had the SIG in his left hand, fumbled the magazine out, pocketed it and put one of the twenty-round magazines in place instead.

"Come on, you cocksuckers!" Saddler shouted. "Eat lead!"

Steel was on his feet, the Uzi in his right fist, the SIG-Sauer P-226 in his left.

The gunfire changed its pattern. There were several semiautomatic shots from the base of the stairwell.

Steel took a gamble, edging out a little from the doorway. Saddler stood framed in the opposite doorway, a gun in each hand, a smile on his face, a cigarette hanging from the left corner of his mouth, the collar of his black leather jacket snapped up, the jacket wide open. The waistband of his trousers bristled with spare magazines for the TEC-9 assault pistol.

"Now, Luther!"

Steel absently thought, Why am I doing what he says? But he stepped into the hallway just as Saddler did, both men spraying out their weapons down the stairwell. Black-clad men with assault rifles fell as they stormed up the stairs. Steel's left side took a hit that he told himself was a grazing wound. Rocky Saddler seemed to stumble.

Saddler advanced to the head of the stairs, Steel doing the same, throwing the last full magazine for the Uzi up the well, dropping the empty to the rubble already littering the hallway floor.

The SIG was empty. No time to reload it.

As one of the attackers charged the steps, Steel fired point blank into the man's abdomen with the Uzi, stepped back, and bashed him across the back of the head again and again with the empty 9mm pistol in his left hand.

Saddler stood at the head of the stairs, firing, hot brass like a corona of light around him.

And suddenly Saddler stopped. At least three men were down that neither Steel nor—as far as he could tell—Rocky Saddler had shot. But they were down and looked dead.

Steel moved to stand beside Saddler.

There was no gunfire from below.

A voice called up. "I'm one of the good guys—don't shoot! I'm coming out, hands up, but I still have my weapons."

Luther Steel experienced the reality of the pain in his left side for the first time and sagged against the stairwell wall.

Saddler shouted, "One wrong move and you're history, pal!"

Where had Steel heard that voice from the bottom of the stairs before?

And he saw the face as Saddler shot a flashlight toward the base of the staircase, Saddler's Browning High Power locked against it.

"He's all right. He's some kind of cop," Steel said.

It was the guy from the conference, the Canadian guy who'd tried to help.

The voice came from the base of the stairs again. "Would you mind terribly turning that light away, my friend?"

CHAPTER NINETEEN

Luther Steel, his wife kneeling beside him, sat at what was left of the kitchen table. Geoffrey Kearney lighted a cigarette, wondering if he'd ever get the chance to sleep.

The local EMTs, as the rather interesting old black fellow had referred to them, would be here in minutes. There wasn't much time to sort things out. Geoffrey Kearney sat across from Steel. Kearney felt a smile starting on his face.

"What's an RCMP guy doing down here?" Luther Steel asked him, visibly wincing as his wife cleaned the wound over his left rib cage, but his voice never wavered.

"That's a good question, Agent Steel. But since I'm not with the RCMP, I couldn't tell you."

"If you're not a Royal Canadian Mountie, what are you?"

"Just a passing traveler who picked up some rather strange radio transmissions and followed them to their source."

The older man—Rocky Saddler—just laughed.

Kearney looked at Saddler. "And you must be the fellow they referred to as the 'Windy City man' —a pleasure to meet you."

"Keep my card, Brit—you might need it." A card appeared from Saddler's left hand as if by magic. The back of his hand was covered with a bandage where he'd been wounded slightly by flying glass. Kearney read the card. "Rocky Saddler—Private Detective." Kearney looked at him as he went to sip at the drink Mrs. Steel had poured for him. "You're British Secret Intelligence Service, pal. I know you won't admit it. But remember something, America's where they invented hardball."

Kearney said nothing.

Neither the unscathed deputy nor the wounded man were present. Mrs. Steel had announced that the wounded marshal seemed to be hanging on, might have a chance. Kearney assumed the one was with the other. The two children sat sharing the same chair near the kitchen counter. Blankets were over the shot-out windows, and the only light came from two flashlights in the center of the table. It was possible, though unlikely, that more of the attackers were still in the woods.

Saddler spoke again. "Luther. I'd say check with

your other agents from the Metro Task Force. See if they're still alive, tell them what happened here. And you're a fool if you wait for the law to arrive."

Kearney merely observed.

"This can't be what you said it was," Steel offered.

"Roman Makowski wants you guys dead so he can nail Rudolph Cerillia to the wall. You can believe it or not. Not a one of those guys who hit us had any ID on him, no labels in the clothes, no serial numbers visible on the guns. Think, man!"

Kearney interrupted. "I assume Mr. Saddler is implying that your new President is out to kill you, Agent Steel. From what he says and from my own observations, it would appear that whoever made the attempt this evening was quite professional, quite dedicated. I'd like to ask you a question. But I'll preface it with a statement. I've always understood that the United States Marshals Service has never lost a cooperating witness under its protection. I assume this was such an operation. Therefore, wouldn't logic suggest that the mere fact that someone found you here—and this was no hastily organized attempt, certainly—indicates that whoever is behind it was privy to government records?"

"Nobody followed us here today, Luther. You can take that to the bank. Not even electronically, because I had the car swept before I picked you up at the airport. And no one followed me out to the airport to do anything while I had it parked. They were waiting for you to arrive, knew when you would arrive, and hit when you were most vulnerable. They had you nailed, Luther. You got off alive this time. So'd your wife and the little guys over there. You've got what they used to call a rich man's family—a beautiful wife and a handsome boy and a beautiful little girl. You want to risk that again?"

"No," Luther Steel barely whispered.

Geoffrey Kearney stood up. "Well, not to drink and run, Mrs. Steel, but I think I'd best be off before those EMT chaps you're awaiting arrive. Too many questions."

"Wait a minute. How do I reach you?" Steel asked, standing, the pain more pronounced in his eyes as he extended his hand. Kearney took it.

Saddler spoke. "If Mr. Kearney here will keep in touch with my service—the line answers twenty-four hours a day—I can handle it."

"Fair enough, Mr. Saddler. I'll do that." And Kearney looked at Steel again. "Call your friends. Warn them. Take this gentleman's advice, Agent Steel. And I will keep in touch. Your country needs men like you—alive, not dead."

Kearney crossed the kitchen, snatched up his rifle from the corner, and walked out.

CHAPTER TWENTY

The most beautiful white swan Thomas Ashbrooke had ever seen seemed to be almost posing on the water. He was a few moments early for his meeting, anyway, and so he stood beside the bank of the little Thames tributary, watching the lovely creature.

Suddenly the bird's graceful neck turned—but only slightly—and the creature swam away. A punt was gliding through the water, just visible as it came from behind the tree cover. In it a young man with flowing blond hair, his white shirt sleeves rolled up and a sleeveless red and whiter sweater over gray slacks, was propelling the broad, low, flat-bottom craft in defiance of the stream. A girl in a pale-blue dress wearing what was likely the man's fedora hat over gorgeously long brown hair was reclining near the prow.

Ashbrooke turned away and walked on along the grassy embankment. Shooting his cuff, he saw that now he was almost a minute late.

As he passed a stand of langorously stretching trees with long, thin, banana-shaped leaves, he saw Millard Pennyworth. "Milly!" Ashbrooke called, but not too loudly.

Pennyworth turned around, doffed his hat, and waved it toward Ashbrooke, then started walking down from the little knoll and toward him. Ashbrooke quickened his pace.

They met at the base of the knoll, a cool breeze the only reminder that it was no longer summer, but fall. "Good to see you, Tom."

"You too, Milly. It's beautiful here."

"Surely you've been up to Oxford before, old man!"

"No," Ashbrooke confided, lighting a cigarette. "I never have. I almost envy you teaching here."

"Yes, it is rather splendid this time of the year, isn't it? But I doubt you traveled all the way from Berlin on such short notice merely to compliment me on one of England's national treasures."

Ashbrooke allowed himself a smile. "I need your help. Are you still connected with—" He didn't quite know how to say it.

"The old-boy network?" Milly supplied, smiling mischieviously. He was six foot or so, painfully thin, and, when he smiled, his face looked like a skull with a stocking of skin stretched too tightly over it.

But there was genuine warmth in his eyes now as there always had been. "Let's walk, shall we?"

"Yes." Ashbrooke nodded, inhaling.

"Actually, you must need something. Because I doubt, old man, that you proposed your question merely for the sake of idle speculation."

"I'm desperately in need of help."

Milly stopped walking, clutched at Ashbrooke's right forearm. "Not your wife—"

"No—Diane's fine."

"I was dreadfully sorry when I heard about Elizabeth—you received my telegram? I thought everyone would be calling and that you would have had enough of that."

"Yes—thanks, Milly."

"If it's not Diane, then—"

"My son-in-law—he works with the Patriots in America. He's been kidnapped by a Russian named Dimitri Borsoi—" Ashbrooke thought he detected some hint of recognition in Milly's eyes but wasn't certain. "It's all tied up with drug smuggling, the KGB, the Front for the Liberation of North America—and I've got to get a meeting arranged with a man named Theron Hyde, the smuggler."

Milly lighted his own cigarette from a slim gold case. "Actually, I've heard of this fellow Hyde, Tom. What do you say to coming round to my office with me? I'll organize us a cup of tea, we can talk a bit more, and then I'll make one or two calls that might assist you. Shall we?"

The wind stopped suddenly. Ashbrooke heard a

bird twittering somewhere. Absently, suddenly, he wondered how the swan was doing.

"I can help, old man—at least I think so," Milly said, taking his arm and starting back toward the knoll.

CHAPTER TWENTY-ONE

There was a telephone outside the convenience store. A sign said that the store was open all night, but it was closed. Nothing was open all night anymore, except police stations and military bases, not since the coming of the FLNA.

The convenience store was located at the junction of two highways, and Luther Steel didn't know which one he should take. Evidently Rocky Saddler did. "I'll wait—make your phone call," Saddler told him.

Steel nodded. His wife, Deana, was in the middle of the backseat of Saddler's car, one child on each side of her. All three of them were asleep.

Steel got out of the car, locked the door and closed it, then walked over to the open telephone booth.

He would make a collect call and pay Clark Pietrowski back for it later. Clark was the senior man
on his Metro Task Force and as he had a house in
Metro he would be the man most likely to— The
phone was picked up on the first ring. "Clark—"

The operator insisted. "I have a collect call for
anyone from Luther."

"I'll take it, Operator," Pietrowski's voice came
back. "Luther—thank God you're alive. Wherever
the hell you're at, you're in deep shit."

"I've just climbed out of some. Clark—look—
they tried—"

"Anna Comacho is dead. Somebody just smoth-
ered her with a damn pillow right there in the hospital while the cop on the door was off takin' a leak. A
truck tried running me over today. I called Runningdeer to tell him about Anna—he was kinda
sweet on her, you know?—and I wound up leaving a
message on his answering machine. He called me
back an hour later. Somebody wired his car with a
bomb, but the thing went off when a parking lot
attendant moved it. There are two guys hanging
around outside my house. I was waiting for you to
call. I'm getting my wife outta here. What are we
gonna do?"

Anna Comacho. The FLNA had thrown acid into
her face to make a point. Now somebody had murdered her in her hospital bed. "You got a way of
contacting Runningdeer?"

"I know where," Pietrowski said, coughing. Steel

could imagine him lighting one of his inevitable cigarettes.

"All right, then. Tell Bill to remember the guy he
and I met just before the election. I'm with him
now. You can contact me through the guy's answering service. We've got to get together, all of us. Can
you check out LeFleur and Blumenthal? Establish a
contact route and tell them to go to ground. Let's
talk in thirty-six hours. I've got things to do here."

"Tell your things—especially the pretty but dumb
one who married you—God bless." The line clicked
dead.

Saddler and the Brit or Canadian or whoever he
was had been right. It had to be someone high up.
And someone who wanted the entire Metro Task
Force out of the way so they could get Rudolph
Cerillia.

For an instant, Steel wondered if Cerillia himself
was in danger. They wouldn't have dared. To pub-
licly discredit him would be more damning than
murdering him.

Luther Steel set down the telephone receiver. He
started back to the car, reminding himself to hold
his head up. He was down, but a long way from out.

Not yet.

CHAPTER TWENTY-TWO

He was up with the sun, checking Maria's temperature first. She seemed fine. If he could keep her level of extertion to a minimum, they would make it. Today.

David Holden had found a good stone and, while he steamed some of the rabbit from the previous evening to warm the meat, he touched up the edge of the Crain Defender knife. "David?"

He stood up from the fire and turned around. "How are you feeling, Maria?"

"We will leave today, no?"

"Yes—we will leave today. It's just a short ride to the river."

"There is a village. Once we reach the river, I can find the direction."

"Good. We'll get a boat there. Then we'll get a

little downriver and wait until nightfall. Then we're home free."

"You are a good man, David. Other men, they might have—" She didn't finish it. He didn't want her to. "You are a good man. You can leave me in the village, if you—"

"No. I'll get you well downriver. Then we can find a safe place for you to stay. Everything will be all right. I thought of who I can reach who can help us. First place we can find in Brazil with international telephone service and we're all set. So just relax. Do you speak Portuguese?" She laughed. It was the first time he'd heard her laugh. It was a very good sound.

They rode well back in the trees, but kept the river in plain sight.

David Holden planned to keep the rifles—all but one—hidden in the trees while he negotiated for a boat. He would much rather part with the horses, but after killing the men to get the horses, he had enough rifles to spare if he had to trade one or two.

Perhaps, he told himself, he could barter for some food and—

The sound came from overhead. A helicopter.

David Holden looked up, reining in on his mount. Maria's horse slammed against his and reared. But she held it under control.

"David?"

"Let's ride!" The helicopter—the Bell Long

Ranger he'd seen before—was zeroing in on them. "Shit!" Holden dug in his heels.

Beside him, Maria shouted to her animal, *"Andele! Andele!"* Either the tree cover hadn't been dense enough or they had merely lain off on the other side of the river, spotted something suspicious, and gone airborne to investigate. "Come on!"

The ground rose dramatically now, Holden's horse nearly pitching him forward as the animal navigated an embankment. Holden glanced back. Maria was a good horsewoman. Her animal was springing up onto the embankment and skidding back slightly. Maria urged the horse ahead.

Holden looked skyward.

The voice of Innocentio Hernandez came from a loud hailer. "Holden! Stop your horse! You cannot escape! Surrender now or be killed!"

The second finger of David Holden's left hand shot skyward as he dug in his heels.

"There is a road, David! Ahead a little!"

Holden didn't like the idea of an open road, but it would make it easier on the animals, and faster. They could pick a likely spot to leave the road, with or without the horses. "Let's go for it!" Holden's right fist held an M-16 and he used the barrel of the assault rifle like a quirt now, raking it across the animal's rump, the horse vaulting ahead. At last, Holden could see the road, the jungle canopy covering it so heavily that only a solitary band of sunlight extended along its center like a dividing line.

Holden's animal jumped a deadfall tree. "Maria
—watch it!"

But her horse was already clear.

They reached another embankment, this time going downward. Holden's horse skidded along it on
its haunches, nearly toppling over, got up and leapt
across the ditch beyond.

Holden reined in for an instant when they
reached the road, the M-16 coming to his shoulder.
As he fired toward the helicopter it cut away, rotating 360 degrees on its axis. There was a flash followed by the crack of high-powered rifle shot, and
in the same instant the roadbed mere yards from his
horse's feet spit up dust.

Holden fired a burst toward the helicopter, but it
was useless, his animal was moving too erratically.
Maria was down the embankment, over the ditch,
urging her horse into the ribbon of sunlight.

Holden spurred his mount after hers.

The helicopter shot out of his peripheral vision
for an instant, and then its roar was almost directly
overhead. Rifles on full automatic hammered lead
into the roadbed on both sides of them. Holden
stabbed his M-16 toward the craft. The helicopter's
shadow hung over him like a black cloud. He fired
out the magazine, then whipped his horse's flanks
with the weapon. The animal galloped into a dead
run and was gaining on Maria's mount. Holden
looked up and back at the helicopter. It had veered
away, but it was coming down on them again.

"David!"

Ahead of them, Holden saw a pickup truck. Men in the bed of the truck scrambled into positions of cover, bringing their rifles up. Holden threw the spent M-16 away, grabbed up a second one tied to his saddle, ripped it from the binding thongs that held it in place, racked the action, and stabbed the rifle toward the men beside the truck. Maria had a pistol in her hand and was firing at them. Holden opened fire. One man was down. Holden's horse faltered as there was a burst of submachine gun fire. The horse stumbled. Holden held on. The animal got to its feet, rearing. Holden fired another burst from the M-16, spraying wildly, his only hope of connecting. Another man was down, his submachine gun firing into the roadbed.

As Maria's horse vaulted past them, the pistol in her hand spit, killing another man. Maria seemed to slump in the saddle as one of the men fired at her.

Holden was even with the truck now, spraying out the M-16 toward the men huddled around it.

Maria's horse slowed. The pistol fell from her hand to the road.

Holden's animal was beside hers and he could see Maria clearly. Her right thigh was splotched bright red with blood. "I am all right—ride, David!"

Holden whacked his rifle across the rear end of her horse, and the animal charged ahead. He changed magazines, firing back at the pickup truck as it started after them, blowing out one of the headlights. Holden fired a useless burst toward the helicopter, wheeled his animal, and dug in his heels.

Ahead, the road took a bend. Maria's horse navigated it safely with Holden's horse at its heels.

The village Maria had spoken of came into view. It was a collection of huts, the jungle encroaching so closely upon the structures as to almost obscure them. And, ahead, he saw the river.

Holden dug in his heels. The water was their only chance.

He heard the voice of Innocentio Hernandez again. "You will die, Holden!" More gunfire blasted from the helicopter. Holden kept riding, the dirt around his horse's feet spraying up under the impacts of the rifle bullets.

They were at the edge of the village square now as another burst of automatic weapons fire came from the helicopter overhead. Maria's horse tumbled forward, spilling Maria from the saddle into the dirt of the road.

Holden rode past, reined in, and jumped down from the saddle. He dropped to one knee, fired the M-16 toward the vanishing gunship, emptying the magazine, and saw a puff of gray-brown smoke near the tail rotor.

The helicopter spun wildly, disappearing under the tree line. The pickup truck was coming right toward them now. Holden ran to Maria, grabbing her up at his left side. "We're gonna make it."

"No—David—no—"

"Come on."

He started to run, the empty M-16 in his right fist, his left arm coiled around Maria's waist.

They had to make it, he told himself.

Villagers were nowhere to be seen. He realized they were hiding from the gunfire. The river was close. Two houses to go and then the little beach area where some of the boats were. If he could get Maria into the water with him, they could hold their breath, swim out of range.

With the helicopter gone—

He looked overhead and saw it. The machine was spewing smoke, and Innocentio Hernandez, hanging out from the right side, held a rifle with a scope on it in his hands.

Heavy assault rifle fire blasted at them.

Holden was almost carrying Maria now. The river.

Gunfire from behind him, from the truck.

Holden let the M-16 fall from his hand, grabbed the Beretta 92F from his waistband, and fired it behind him.

Maria fell.

Holden wheeled toward the truck, firing out the Beretta. The windshield of the pickup spider-webbed, shattered, and the pickup veered away from him, impacting into one of the village houses, the house collapsing around it.

"David!"

Holden turned to Maria.

Above him, he heard the voice of Innocentio Hernandez. "You die!"

Holden threw himself toward Maria, grabbed for

her as bullets ripped along the center of the square. Holden pulled her up, clutching her against him, and ran.

Gunfire tore into the ground at his feet. Holden stumbled. Maria was on her knees.

More gunfire. Maria threw herself over him as the helicopter's shadow streaked away.

As Holden pushed up, Maria crumpled away from him. Her eyes were open. Blood trickled from her mouth.

"Maria—"

She smiled and closed her eyes, but they opened in the next instant.

"Maria."

Holden touched at her throat. There was no pulse. She was staring into the sun.

Holden got to his knees. He rammed a fresh magazine into the Beretta.

The helicopter. David Holden stabbed the pistol toward it, firing, firing, the slide locking open, the pistol empty.

"Son of a bitch!"

David Holden looked once more at Maria. "I'll get him for you. So help me God, Maria."

Holden ran for the water, gunfire furrowing the ground around him, past the boats, still clutching the pistol, running into the water, up to his waist, as the water sprayed up around him as bullets impacted its surface.

He dove forward and down.

* * *

David Holden shivered. He had stayed in the water until nightfall, when Innocentio Hernandez's men had stopped searching.

He'd seen Hernandez. Hernandez still limped from the bullet wound Holden had given him as a parting gift when he'd escaped the villa.

When at last they had given up, Holden had stayed in the water for another hour.

He swam out to the opposite shore.

He sat on a log that wasn't termite infested. The sun had set and with the darkness came the cold.

With dry leaves, he wiped off the Beretta, wiped off the magazines and the cartridges.

Then he took the Defender knife from the sodden rag sheath he had made for it.

David Holden held the knife tight in his fist. He looked at the purpling darkness and whispered, "I won't forget, Maria. I promise I won't. He's a dead man."

GREAT BOOKS

E-BOOKS

AUDIOBOOKS

& MORE

Visit us today

www.speakingvolumes.us

www.ingramcontent.com/pod-product-compliance
Lightning Source LLC
Chambersburg PA
CBHW050737250626
47155CB00005B/1816